A NEST
of VIPERS

Center Point
Large Print

Also by Andrea Camilleri and available from
Center Point Large Print:

The Brewer of Preston
Game of Mirrors
A Beam of Light
A Voice in the Night

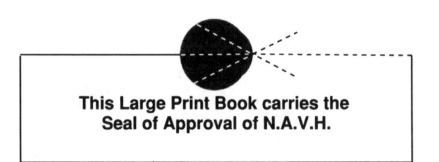

**This Large Print Book carries the
Seal of Approval of N.A.V.H.**

A NEST
of VIPERS

Andrea Camilleri
Translated by Stephen Sartarelli

CENTER POINT LARGE PRINT
THORNDIKE, MAINE

This Center Point Large Print edition
is published in the year 2017 by arrangement with
Penguin Books, an imprint of Penguin Publishing Group,
a division of Penguin Random House LLC.

Originally published in Italian as *Un covo di vipere*
by Sellerio Editore, Palermo.

The text of this Large Print edition is unabridged.
In other aspects, this book may vary
from the original edition.
Printed in the United States of America
on permanent paper.
Set in 16-point Times New Roman type.

ISBN: 978-1-68324-552-0

Library of Congress Cataloging-in-Publication Data

Names: Camilleri, Andrea, author. | Sartarelli, Stephen, 1954– translator.
Title: A nest of vipers / Andrea Camilleri ; translated by Stephen Sartarelli.
Description: Center Point Large Print edition. | Thorndike, Maine :
    Center Point Large Print, 2017.
Identifiers: LCCN 2017028429 | ISBN 9781683245520
    (hardcover : alk. paper)
Subjects: LCSH: Montalbano, Salvo (Fictitious character)—Fiction. |
    Large type books. | BISAC: FICTION / Mystery & Detective / General. |
    FICTION / Suspense. | GSAFD: Mystery fiction | Suspense fiction
Classification: LCC PQ4863.A3894 C68 2017b | DDC 853/.914—dc23
LC record available at https://lccn.loc.gov/2017028429

1

He found himself in a dense forest with Livia, having no idea how they got there. That it was a virgin forest there could be no doubt, because some ten yards back they'd seen a wooden sign nailed to a tree with the words *Virgin Forest* etched in fire. The two of them looked like Adam and Eve, in that they were completely naked but for their pudenda, which, though there was nothing to be ashamed about, they'd covered with classic fig leaves they'd bought for one euro at a stand at the entrance to the forest. But since these were made of plastic, and rather stiff, they were a bit uncomfortable, though the biggest bother was having to walk barefoot.

As Montalbano advanced, he became more and more convinced that he'd been in that place before. But when? The head of a lion, glimpsed through the trees—which weren't trees but gigantic ferns—provided the explanation.

"Know where we are, Livia?"

"Yes, in a virgin forest. I saw the sign."

"But it's a painted forest!"

"What do you mean, 'painted'?"

"We're inside *The Dream*, the famous painting by the Douanier Rousseau!"

"Have you lost your mind?"

"You'll see I'm right. Soon we'll be running into Yadwigha."

"And how do you know this woman?" Livia asked suspiciously.

Indeed, moments later they ran into Yadwigha, who was lying there naked on her litter; upon seeing them she brought a forefinger to her lips, enjoining them to be silent, and said:

"It's about to begin."

A bird, perhaps a nightingale, landed on a branch, made a sort of bow to the guests, and launched into "Il cielo in una stanza."

The bird was an excellent singer, a pure delight, performing modulations even Mina couldn't pull off. He was clearly improvising, but with the fancy of a true artist.

Then there was a loud boom, then another, then a third louder than the first two, and Montalbano woke up.

Cursing the saints, he realized that a huge storm had broken out. One of those that signaled the end of the summer.

But how was it that, despite all the racket, he could still hear, even awake, the bird singing "Il cielo in una stanza"? It wasn't possible.

He got up and looked at the clock. Six-thirty in the morning. He headed for the veranda. That was where the whistling was coming from. And it wasn't a bird, but a man who could whistle like a bird. Montalbano opened the French door.

Lying on the veranda was a man of about fifty, poorly dressed in a threadbare jacket, with a beard so long he looked like Moses, and a mass of disheveled, ashen hair. And beside him, a bag. A vagabond, clearly.

As soon as he saw Montalbano, he sat up and said:

"Did I wake you up? I'm sorry. I came here to take cover from the rain. If it's a bother, I'll go."

"No, no, you can stay," said the inspector.

He was struck by the way the man spoke. Aside from his perfect grammar, he had a polite tone that made an impression.

It would have seemed rude to shut the French door in the man's face, and so the inspector left it half open and went to make a pot of coffee.

He'd already drunk his first mugful when he began to feel a little guilty. He poured another mugful and took it out to the man.

"For me?" the other asked in astonishment, rising to his feet.

"Yes."

"Thank you! Thank you so much!"

As the inspector was enjoying his shower, it occurred to him that the poor bastard probably hadn't bathed in God knows how long. When he finished, he went back out on the veranda. The rain was coming down hard.

"Would you like to take a shower?"

The man looked at him, at a loss for words.

"Are you serious?"

"I'm serious."

"It's all I ever dream about. You have no idea how grateful I am for this."

No, the man spoke too well to be what he appeared to be. The stranger bent down to pick up his bag and followed the inspector. But if he was an educated man, how had he ended up in such a state?

When the man came out of the bathroom, he'd changed his shirt, but this one, too, had a frayed collar and cuffs. He smiled at Montalbano.

"I feel twenty years younger," he said.

Then, with a slight bow:

"Savastano's the name, if I may."

"A pleasure to meet you. I'm Montalbano," said the inspector, holding out his hand.

Before shaking it, the man made an instinctive gesture, rubbing his palm on his trouser leg, as if to clean it. He smiled again, revealing a gap where a tooth was missing in front.

"I know who you are, you know. One night, in a bar, I saw you on television."

"Listen," said Montalbano, "I have to go to the office now."

The man understood at once. He bent down to pick up his bag and went out onto the veranda.

"Do you mind, Inspector, if I stay here until it stops raining? My home, so to speak, is just a stone's throw away, but in this rain . . . But you go ahead and lock up."

"Listen, if you want I can give you a ride."

"Thanks, but that would be rather difficult."

"Why?"

"Because I live in a cave halfway up the hill of marl directly behind your house."

Well, living inside a cave was still better than lying down under the columned portico of city hall with cardboard boxes for blankets.

"You can stay as long as you like. Have a good day."

He reached into his pocket for his wallet, took out a twenty-euro note, and held it out to the man.

"No, thank you. You've already done so much for me," the man said decisively.

Montalbano didn't insist.

As he closed the French door he heard the man whistling again. He was good, damned good. Almost as good as the bird in his dream.

The moment the inspector set foot in the station, Catarella set down his telephone receiver and yelled:

"Ahh, Chief, Chief! I's jess tryin' a call yiz a' 'ome!"

"Why, what is it?"

" 'Ere's a moider, 'a'ss what! Fazio jess now wint to the scene o' the crime! An' 'e wannit yiz to go to the scene where 'e's onna scene! Ann' 'a'ss why I's callin' yiz a' 'ome foist ting inna mornin'!"

"Okay, fine, where's this place?"

"I writ it down onna piss o' paper. 'Ere it is. Villino Pariella, in Tosacane districk."

"And where is this Villino Pariella?"

"In Tosacane districk, Chief."

"Yes, but where's this district?"

"Dunno, Chief."

"Listen, get Fazio on the line and put the call through to me."

Following Fazio's instructions, he got to Villino Mariella—Catarella would never manage to get a name right, not in a million years—after some forty-five minutes at the wheel, since there was a lot of traffic and the rain kept falling hard from the heavens and slowed the circulation down.

It was a two-story house right on the road that ran along the beach. The gate was open, and under the arcade there was a police car beside two other cars. Since he didn't want to get wet, as it was still raining cats and dogs, he drove up and parked beside the other cars.

He was about to get out of the car when Fazio came up to the window.

"Good morning, Chief."

"Does it seem so good to you?"

"No, it's just a way to say hello."

10

"What happened here?"

"Ragioniere Cosimo Barletta, the owner of the house, was murdered."

"Who's inside?"

"Gallo, the dead man, and his son Arturo, who discovered the body."

"Have you informed everyone?"

"Yessir. Five minutes ago."

Montalbano went into the house, with Fazio following behind.

In the first room, which was rather large and clearly furnished as a dining room, were Gallo and a fortyish man with glasses, thin and anonymous looking—that is, possessed of one of those faces that you forget the moment you see it. He was well dressed, perfectly neat, smoking a cigarette, and didn't look the least bit chagrined by what had just happened to his father.

"I'm Arturo Barletta," he said.

"I'm sorry, but who's Mariella?" asked Montalbano.

The man gave him a confused look.

"I don't know . . . I couldn't say . . ."

"I'm sorry, I only asked because the house is called Villino Mariella . . ."

Arturo Barletta slapped himself in the forehead.

"Ah, you know, at moments like these one doesn't . . . Mariella was my poor mother's name."

"Is she dead?"

"Yes. She died five years ago. A terrible accident."

"What kind of accident?"

"She drowned in the sea. She may have had some kind of malaise while swimming. It was right here in front of the house."

"Where is he?" Montalbano asked Fazio.

"In the kitchen. Come."

In the living room there was a staircase leading upstairs, a door on the right leading to the kitchen, and another door, on the left, leading to a bathroom.

The kitchen was spacious, and it looked as if the house's inhabitants normally ate there.

It was in perfect order except for an overturned cup on the table, out of which some coffee had spilled onto the tablecloth, staining it.

The late ragioniere Cosimo Barletta had been killed while sitting sideways, drinking his coffee, which his killer hadn't given him time to finish.

A single shot at the base of the skull, point-blank.

Like an execution.

The shot had knocked him out of his chair, and the body now lay on the floor on its side, with its feet under the table. To look at the man's face, the inspector had to lie down, too. But there wasn't much to see: The bullet, after entering the back of his neck, had come out above the nose, taking with it one eye and part of the forehead. Surely the killer, unless he was a midget, had held the barrel tilted slightly upwards; otherwise there would have been a different trajectory.

There wasn't much blood on the floor, however.

The inspector went back into the dining room. Arturo was chain-smoking.

"Please sit down. I'd like to ask you a few questions."

"That's what I'm here for."

"I'm told it was you who discovered your father's body."

"Yes."

"Tell me how it happened."

"I live in Montelusa and . . ."

"What do you do?"

"I work as an accountant for a large construction firm called Sicilian Spring. Do you know it?"

"No. Are you married?"

"Yes."

"Any children?"

"No."

"Go on."

"Papa and I used to talk on the phone every day. Last night he called me to let me know that he was coming here to sleep because he wanted to put the house in order this morning."

"Put it in order how?"

"Well, since summer's over, he—"

"He never came here in the winter?"

"Of course he did! Every Saturday. But since

13

my sister had recently been here with her two children, he thought it might be a little messy, and my father was a very—"

"What's your sister's name?"

"Giovanna. She's married to a traveling salesman and also lives in Montelusa."

"Go on."

"Well, Papa rang me last night and—"

"What time last night?"

"A little past nine. He'd already eaten at his place in Vigàta and—"

"Did he remarry?"

"No."

"Did he live alone?"

"Yes."

"How old was he?"

"Sixty-three."

"Go on."

"What was I saying? You know, you keep interrupting me, and so I—"

"You were saying that your father called you after nine o'clock."

"Ah, yes. And he told me he would be sleeping here. And so I said I would come here to give him a hand."

"With your wife?"

Arturo Barletta looked a little embarrassed.

"My father didn't really get along with—"

"I see. And so?"

"So I got here this morning at eight and—"

14

"By car?"

"Yes. The green one. The purple one is Papa's. The door was locked. I opened it with my key and—"

"Does your sister also have a key?"

"Yes, I think so."

"When you came in, did you notice anything strange?"

"No . . . I'm sorry, I mean, yes."

"And what was that?"

"I noticed that the shutters were closed and the light was on. But I thought that Papa must still be asleep and had just forgotten to turn it off. I went upstairs. The bed was unmade, but he wasn't in it. So I went back downstairs, went into the kitchen, and saw him."

"What did you do?"

"I don't understand."

"What did you do? Did you start screaming? Did you run up to your father to see if he was still alive? Or did you do something else?"

"I don't remember whether I screamed or not. I'm quite sure I didn't touch him, however."

"Why not? I would think that's an instinctive reaction."

"Yes, but, you see, I needed only to bend down and look at him to . . . Half his face was gone and I immediately realized that he couldn't . . ."

"Just tell me what you did."

15

"I ran out of the kitchen. I couldn't stand the . . . Then I came in here and called you."

"With that?" asked Montalbano, indicating a telephone sitting on a small table.

"Yes."

"You said that the moment you entered you noticed the light was on. Do you remember whether it was also on in the kitchen?"

"I think it was."

"It had to have been, since the shutters are closed."

"Then I guess it was on."

"Shall we go upstairs?" Montalbano asked Fazio.

They climbed the staircase.

Upstairs were two bedrooms with double beds, a smaller room equipped with a bunk bed, and a bathroom. In the first of the large bedrooms the bed was unmade, just as Arturo had said.

He had forgotten to mention, however, that it clearly looked as if two people had slept in that bed.

The two other rooms were tidy, but in the bathroom there were two large towels, still damp. So two people had taken a shower.

They went back downstairs to the dining room.

"Did your father have a lover?"

"Not that I know of."

"Well, the fact is that someone slept here with him last night. Didn't you see the bed?"

"Yes, but I hadn't noticed."

"Listen, don't take offense, but the person your father slept with wasn't necessarily a woman."

Arturo Barletta gave a hint of a smile.

"My father only liked women."

"But you just told me he didn't have any lovers!"

"Because I thought you meant a steady lover. He was . . . Well, let's just say he never missed an opportunity. And he liked 'em young. It was the cause of many quarrels between him and my sister."

"What did your father do for a living?"

Arturo Barletta hesitated a moment.

"A lot of things."

"Tell me a couple."

"Well . . . he had a wholesale lumber store . . . he was a partner in a supermarket venture . . . he owned ten or so rental apartments in Vigàta as well as Montelusa . . ."

"So he was rich."

"Let's say he was well-off."

"Could you have a look around and tell me if anything is missing?"

"I already did, when I was waiting for you. I didn't notice anything missing."

"Did he have any enemies?"

"Well . . . I wouldn't rule that out."

"Why?"

"My father was not an easy man. And when he

17

did business, he didn't care about anybody but himself."

"I see."

The inspector paused, then turned to Fazio.

"Are there any signs of a break-in on the door or any of the windows?"

"None, Chief."

"So Papa must have let the person in," Arturo cut in.

Montalbano looked at him thoughtfully.

"Do you really think so? It could have been the person sleeping with your father who let him in. Nor can we rule out the possibility that the killer had the key."

Arturo Barletta said nothing.

"Please give Fazio your address and phone numbers, and your sister's too," said the inspector.

Then, turning to Fazio:

"I'm going back to the office. You wait here for the prosecutor and the others. I'll see you later. Have a good day."

Outside it was raining harder than before.

2

"Get me Inspector Augello," the inspector said to Catarella as he walked past the closet that served as both guard booth and switchboard. Catarella leapt to his feet and stood at attention.

" 'E in't onna premisses, Chief."

"But did he show up this morning?"

" 'E showed ann'enn 'e unshowed, Chief, like a flashin' flash o' lightnin', in so much as 'e come in ann'enn 'e left. 'E was abliged."

"In what sense?"

"Inna sense 'at summon called 'ere atta swishboard all rilly oigentlike an' askin' oigently f'r'elp 'cuz of a rape of a frog."

"Somebody was raping a frog?"

"Azackly. A fimminine frog, Chief. A froggess."

How was that possible?

"Was the phone call recorded?"

"Natcherly, Chief."

"Lemme hear it."

Catarella fiddled with some keys and soon the agitated voice of a probably elderly woman could be heard saying she'd called because she was witnessing *a rape in progress*.

In a way, despite the fact that the inspector felt instinctively like killing rapists whenever they came within range, he relaxed a little.

If it had really involved a frog, it would have meant that humanity—already brilliantly well on its way—was dangerously accelerating its journey towards total madness.

He went into his room and sat down, discouraged, looking at the huge stack of papers to be signed on his desk.

It occurred to him that bureaucracy across the world was most certainly contributing to the end of that same world. How many forests had been cut down over the years to make the paper necessary for all these useless bureaucratic memos?

And not immediately answering a letter from the administration was worse, because they would be sure to send another letter of reminder concerning the memo not dispatched. Not dispatched! So, if he answered it, then the memo would be dispatched.

Criminals used the same word, *dispatch,* to mean "to kill someone." Therefore the bureaucracy could be likened to a gigantic criminal organization, a kind of ubiquitous Mafia. No wonder a real revolutionary like Che Guevara was so against bureaucracy!

Resigned, the inspector grabbed a ballpoint pen and the file at the top of the pile.

Around midday, by which time his right arm had grown numb from all the signing, he told Catarella to call Fazio's cell phone.

"Where are you?"

Before answering, Fazio heaved a long sigh.

"Still here at the house, Chief."

"What's taking so long?"

"Hello? Are you there, Chief?"

"Hello! What's wrong, can't you hear me?"

"Wait a second while I go outside. The reception's not very good in here."

It was just an excuse. Obviously he didn't want the other people in the room to hear him.

"You there, Chief?"

"Yeah, tell me everything."

"Prosecutor Tommaseo got here about five minutes ago. He'd gone and crashed into a gasoline pump, and since he broke his glasses, after the pump he crashed straight into a tractor-trailer parked in the lot."

It was well known that Tommaseo behind the wheel was a genuine menace to public safety. Though he drove at only ten miles an hour, he was still capable of doing damage.

"To say nothing of the curses and obscenities coming from Dr. Pasquano when he had to wait all that time just to move the corpse."

"Listen, did Barletta leave you those addresses and phone numbers?"

"Yessir."

"Give the sister a ring. Tell me her name again."

"Giovanna."

21

"Tell her to come to the station this afternoon at four o'clock."

He'd just hung up when Mimì Augello, his second-in-command, came in.

"What's this about a rape?" the inspector asked him.

"Some lady, Assuntina Naccarato by name, looked out her window and saw some guy trying to rape a girl, who was crying desperately, in the bedroom of the house in front. And so she called us."

"You got there too late, naturally."

"Way too late. The rapist had already had his way with the girl and was gone. The girl, who was still crying, told me she didn't recognize the guy, who she said was black and had entered the house through the front door, which had been left unlocked."

"Did you question the neighbor lady?"

"Signora Naccarato? Of course."

"And did she confirm?"

"Are you kidding? Assuntina Naccarato claims the rapist not only wasn't black, but was a white man she had no problem recognizing."

"Explain."

"According to Signora Assuntina, this rape is, so to speak, a regular occurrence."

"A regular occurrence?" said Montalbano, appalled.

"It's like this. For the past three months or so,

22

the girl's uncle, her father's brother, comes to the house every week when nobody else is there and takes advantage of her. You should know that the girl is sort of a half-wit. This time, however, she rebelled so loudly that Signora Assuntina felt obliged to call the police."

"And why didn't she call us all the other times?"

"She said she didn't want to meddle. But this time the girl went nuts, and so . . ."

"Apparently the signora's sense of morality functions according to decibel levels. But it's so strange!"

"What's so strange?"

"That the rapist wasn't a Third World foreigner."

"What are you saying!"

"It's not me saying it. Just yesterday evening I heard the chief editor of the news argue that while it's wrong for Italians to slaughter a Congolese or send a Chinese to the hospital, we must nevertheless bear in mind that *all* rapes of Italian women—and he stressed the word *all* with his tone of voice—are committed by non-Europeans. So what are we going to do about it?"

"I guess I'll write in the report that Antonio Sferlazza—that's the uncle's name—is of remote North African origin," said Augello.

"Did you arrest him?"

"Yes."

"Where is he now?"

"Here, in the holding cell. I'm waiting for a crew from Montelusa Prison to come and get him. Want me to bring him here to you?"

"I wouldn't dream of it. I might feel tempted to kick him in the teeth."

He went out to Enzo's trattoria. Seeing that it would surely keep raining until nightfall and that he would not, therefore, be able to take his customary digestive-meditative walk along the jetty out to the lighthouse, he decided not to eat much.

"What can I get you?"

"Enzo, I'd like to keep to light stuff. No first courses. Bring me—"

"What a shame!"

"Why?"

"Because today my wife made spaghetti with mussels and clams and had the good idea to give it a touch of hot pepper and another condiment that she wouldn't reveal to me. It's a real miracle, believe me!"

"I'll have some," the inspector said without hesitation.

In the end, he ate even more than usual.

But when he came out of the restaurant, he felt better prepared to face the rest of the gray, rainy day.

                              • • •

He found Fazio at the station.

"Have you had lunch?"

"Yessir."

"Then have a seat. What did Pasquano tell you?"

"You know what the doctor's like, don't you? This time, with the prosecutor coming so late, his usual bad mood was multiplied by a hundred."

"I can imagine."

"It was absolutely impossible to say anything to him. If I had, he was liable to bite my head off."

"I'll give him a ring tomorrow or go and see him. Let's hope his poker game goes well at the club tonight. That'll make him more manageable. Now tell me what else happened, aside from Pasquano being rude to everyone."

"Well, Chief, on Barletta's side of the bed, Forensics found three long strands of hair, female and naturally blond."

"But shouldn't they have been on the pillow on the other side of the bed?"

Fazio seemed embarrassed.

"Chief, apparently the woman moved over, because . . . and she had her face over Barletta's stomach when he probably grabbed a tight hold of her head and pulled out a few hairs . . . Get the picture?"

"Perfectly."

"Then Pasquano told Arquà he wanted Forensics to test the coffee that had spilled onto the tablecloth and what was left in the cup with the undissolved sugar."

Montalbano looked puzzled.

"Did he explain why?"

"No."

"But if Barletta was killed by a shot to the base of the skull, what's the coffee got to do with it?"

"No idea."

"Listen, I want you to be here with me when Barletta's daughter comes in. But when we're done, as soon as she leaves, you have to go hunting. I want to know everything there is to know about Barletta and his son."

"Whatever you say, Chief."

"And I also want you to try and find out who the blonde woman sleeping beside him was."

"That'll be a little harder."

"Try anyway."

Giovanna Barletta Pusateri was a very attractive woman of about thirty-five who was keen, though there was no need, on appearing a few years younger than her age. Perhaps she wished time had stopped ten years earlier. She was tall and blonde with hazel eyes with green highlights, long legged and elegant in her designer jeans. Montalbano, caught off guard, gawked at her for a few seconds. Fazio, too, seemed a little dazed.

Unlike her brother Arturo, she was clearly grief stricken by her father's death. Her eyes were teary and her hands shook. But she controlled herself.

As soon as she sat down, the inspector asked her:

"Why didn't your husband come?"

Giovanna seemed surprised.

"I wasn't told to bring him. And anyway . . ."

Montalbano cast a questioning glance at Fazio, who threw up his hands.

"Chief, nobody told me . . ."

"Okay, okay, I'll see him tomorrow morning."

Giovanna shook her head no.

"That's what I was about to say. Carlo's not in Montelusa. He's out and about on business. He's gone and won't be back until the day after tomorrow."

"Do you have children?"

"Two. One is thirteen, the other eleven."

"When did you last see your father?"

"A week ago. I would come down to Vigàta once a week, usually on days when Carlo was definitely not around."

"Did you have more time on such days, with your husband not around?"

"That wasn't the only reason, Inspector. Carlo and Papa didn't . . . they didn't get along."

"Can you tell me why?"

"I married Carlo against my father's wishes. In

27

fact, I might as well tell you everything before someone else does. I left my parents' home when I was twenty to go live with Carlo. My father was adamant and always saying that Carlo was a good-for-nothing, so I had no choice. We got married two years later, but Papa didn't come to the wedding. Finally, in the end he forgave me and we started seeing each other again. Sometimes I would spend the night at his place."

"What about the children?"

"There's the nanny."

The nanny? And those designer jeans? How much did a traveling salesman make, anyway?

"Listen, who was it that broke the news to you?"

"The news of Papa's death? Arturo, of course."

"When?"

"This morning. I don't remember at what time. It must have been around half past seven."

"Are you sure about that?"

"Well, give or take a few minutes. Gianni and Cosimo, my two boys, had just finished eating breakfast."

"I see. Do you know whether your father had any enemies?"

"Of course he did."

"Give me a few names."

She gave him a tense smile. She was a truly beautiful woman, with a mouth that immediately gave one ideas.

"I think the list would be pretty long. Papa was . . . was not an easy person, and in matters of business he didn't pull any punches."

Basically the same thing her brother Arturo had said.

"And how were his relations with your brother?"

"At first they were excellent. Then, three years ago, there was a rift."

"Do you know the reason?"

"Of course. The will."

"Meaning?"

"One Sunday—it was summer—Papa invited Arturo and me to the beach house for lunch. He didn't want me to bring the children. At the end of the meal, he told us he was planning to make a will. And he gave us advance notice that the greater part of the inheritance would come to me. Arturo took it badly and demanded an explanation. Papa replied that it was because I had two children and he had none. Arturo got up from the table and left. Later they made peace, but their relationship was never quite the same after that."

"And, as far as you know, did he make the will in the end?"

"I honestly don't know."

"Did he have a notary?"

"Yes, a very good friend of his. Named Piscopo, from Montelusa."

"Here's a delicate question. Did your father have a lover?"

"No."

"So, in your opinion, after the tragic death of his wife, he no longer—"

Another smile, even more forced than the previous one.

"That's not what I meant. My father was a full-blooded, vital man. He just didn't have a steady lover. But he certainly had plenty of girls!"

Again, the brother and sister were saying the same thing.

"Girls?"

"Yes, he liked them young."

"How young?"

"Don't get the wrong idea. He wasn't a pedophile. He liked twenty-year-olds."

"Did he ever mention any of their names to you?"

"Anna, Giuliana, Vittoria . . ."

"I'm sorry, but why would girls so young go with a man so much older than them?"

"Papa was a very charismatic older man. He made a point of staying in shape and he dressed well. And, on top of that . . ."

"Tell me."

"He was very generous with them. Arturo would often quarrel with him specifically over—"

She suddenly broke off.

"Go on."

"I wouldn't want you to misunderstand."

"I won't."

"They were family quarrels of a very common sort. Not big scenes. Arturo would reproach him for squandering his money on young girls."

"And what would your father say?"

"He would tell him not to worry, that after he died there would be plenty left over for him in the safe. But there was something else Arturo feared, and he wanted me as his ally. But I didn't want to get involved."

"What was your brother afraid of?"

"That Papa would lose his head over one of those girls."

"And so?"

"To be more precise: He was afraid Papa would fall in love and change the will. And he told me that if this happened, I too would lose my inheritance."

"I get it. And I have to tell you that your father wasn't alone in that house on his last night."

"He wasn't?"

"No."

"Who was with him?"

"A blonde woman."

"How do you know that?"

"Our forensics team found some long blond hair in the bed."

31

"But couldn't it have been there from before?"

"What do you mean?"

"Papa didn't have a cleaning woman for that house. Or, actually, he did have one who would go there and tidy up now and then in the off-season. Papa took care of everything himself, and he made his own bed himself, though often he would merely pull up the sheet. So what I mean is that the hair might have been there from before last night."

Her reasoning made perfect sense.

"Anyway, why is that so important?" she continued. "I've just finished telling you that Papa—"

"It's important, believe me. Since there are no signs of forced entry, it might have been that woman who let the killer in."

Giovanna opened her eyes wide.

"Do you really think so?"

"It's a possibility."

"My God, that's horrible!"

"Do you know who your father was currently seeing?"

"I may be mistaken, but when I was at his place a little less than two months ago, the phone rang and I answered. It was a woman, and she sounded young. She said her name was Stella and she wanted to talk to Papa."

"Did you hear any of their conversation?"

"I couldn't help it. Papa told her he would wait

for her as he always did, at the usual hour. And he hung up."

"And you know nothing else about this Stella?"

"I do. I jokingly asked Papa who his new flame was, and he answered that she was a medical student who lived with her parents here in Vigàta. But that's all I can tell you."

Montalbano stood up, and Fazio did likewise.

"Thank you, you've been very helpful. I'll give you a call if I need you for anything else. Fazio, please accompany the lady."

Who, viewed from behind, didn't lose a thing. On the contrary. Fazio returned.

"Do you know the first thing you must do?" Montalbano asked.

"Yes."

"Tell me."

"Find out the surname of a certain medical student named Stella."

3

The rain had stopped, but the humidity outside got into one's bones.

Since there was no point in eating on the veranda, he just sat there for a few minutes gazing at the sea. Way out on the water were a few fishing lamps, since nowadays the fish stayed well away from the stinking, polluted shore. He went inside and set the table in the kitchen.

Adelina, his housekeeper, had left him a platter of seafood salad in the fridge, enough for three people and more. He conscientiously scarfed down the whole thing, and when he was done, since he still felt hungry, he made himself a hefty plate of passuluna olives and bread, which he went and ate standing up, leaning against the jamb of the French door. After a day's work he always needed to breathe in the air of the sea to clean out his lungs and mind.

Then, leaving the French door ajar, he went and sat in the armchair and turned on the TV. He channel-surfed until he found a film he'd seen before but had rather liked: *Bad Lieutenant*. He watched it again and then switched to the TeleVigàta news broadcast.

Naturally, the most important news item was

the murder of Ragioniere Barletta. There was nothing said in the report that the inspector didn't already know.

The only new thing was the interview with Barletta's son at the end of the feature. Arturo repeated what he'd already said, but at a certain point, when the interviewer asked him if he had any idea who might have killed his father, he said:

> There were officially four sets of keys to the house: one in my possession; the second in my sister's; the third was found in my father's pocket; and the fourth, the extra set, is at my father's place in town. I checked myself. Since the killer entered without forcing the door, there are two possibilities: Either the killer used one of those four sets, or my father let him in.

At this point the interviewer made a strange face and said:

> I'm sorry, but going by what you say, if we put aside the hypothesis that it was your father who opened the door, do you realize that you and your sister then become prime suspects?

Arturo looked at him and smiled.

I'm well aware of that, but that's the simple reality. We mustn't rule out, however, that there may be other sets of keys that my father had made and gave to persons outside the family.

The interviewer:

And why would he have had such copies made?

Arturo, throwing up his hands:

I really wouldn't know.

Montalbano lolled about the house for half an hour, awaiting Livia's call, which came a few minutes before midnight.

Her voice sounded cheerful.

"Listen, Salvo. By a totally unexpected stroke of luck, I've been freed up to come and spend some time with you in Vigàta. I could get there the day after tomorrow. What do you think?"

"I await you with open arms. Though at the moment I can't promise you I'll have the time to come and get you at Palermo Airport."

"Are you really busy?"

"A murder was discovered this morning."

"A woman?"

"No, a man. What made you think the victim might be a woman?"

"Because it's become fashionable in Italy to kill women. Did you know this man?"

"No. But, at any rate, I think I'm going to be rather busy in the coming days."

"That's okay. It's enough for me if you come home in the evening."

"That, you can count on. But, listen, something strange happened to me this morning. I was having this dream, and you were in it with me . . ."

And he told her, in great detail, about the hobo on the veranda and the strong impression the man had made on him.

"So he refused the money you wanted to give him?"

"Yes."

"What was he like?"

"In what sense?"

"Was he tall, short, fat, thin . . . ?"

"Basically similar in build to me."

"Listen, you have at least two shirts that you've never worn because they were presents from Adelina and not to your taste. And you also have a suit, the brown one, which you've stopped wanting to wear because there's a stain on the left sleeve of the jacket. And there's even a pair of shoes, the English ones, that you say hurt your feet . . . Pack all that stuff up and take it to the guy in his cave."

37

There was one problem, however.

"Okay. But not the shirts from Adelina."

"Why not? Do you like them now? Have your tastes changed?"

"No, my tastes haven't changed, but if Adelina realizes I've given them away, there'll be a *catunio* here."

"And what's that mean?"

"Adelina will get upset."

"Well, let her get upset! You let that woman do whatever the hell she wants!"

The two women didn't get along. In fact, they couldn't stand the sight of each other. So whenever Livia came, Adelina would disappear and not come back until Livia was gone.

"Listen, Livia."

"No! As soon as anyone touches your Adelina, you—"

"Come on, Livia, don't be silly!"

"You're the silly one! You don't even realize you've let her run our household!"

"That's just bullshit!"

"What did you say?"

Having come to this point, there was no way the conversation couldn't end up in the gutter. Which is exactly what happened.

After hanging up, he went and opened the armoire. He took out his brown suit and a shirt he'd already decided not to wear anymore, and laid them down on the bed. Then he went into the bathroom and took the English shoes from the shoe rack and put them in a plastic bag. Then he put everything in a large tailor's bag, one of those that Adelina collected and stored in the closet.

Finally he closed the French door, took a shower, and went to bed.

The morning promised a day so clear and bright that it seemed to be apologizing for the gloom of the day before.

When he came out of the house with the bag in his hand, he stopped and looked at the hill of white marl that stood across the road to Vigàta. He immediately noticed the mouth of the cave halfway up the slope. One reached it by way of a narrow path that luckily was not too steep.

Montalbano had a little trouble crossing the road, due to the already considerable traffic, then climbed the path up the hill.

He stopped at the cave's entrance.

"Anyone here?"

No answer. He bent down and went in.

There was enough light inside to see that the man was not there. Either he hadn't returned or had already gone out.

The cave had been furnished. There was a straw mattress for sleeping, a small, broken table, a wicker chair with the seat half caved in, and an oil lamp. In one corner were a number of cardboard boxes stuck together with adhesive tape. The inspector put his bag on the table, went back down the path, crossed the street, got in his car, and drove off.

He'd just sat down in his office and was looking disconsolately at the stack of papers, which had mysteriously grown taller than he remembered, when the telephone rang.

"Ahh, Chief! 'Ere'd happen a be a goil 'at'd like to talk t'yiz poissonally in poisson, an' she sez it evolves a rilly oigently oigent matter."

"Did she tell you her name?"

"Yessir, she did, bu' I din't get it. She tol' me, the goil did, 'at she's called a sister."

"What? And she has no name?"

"Nah, Chief. She's jess called 'sister.' Mebbe she's a nun."

"Okay, send her in."

The girl who entered was about twenty, of medium height with long blond hair, an angelic face, and a body that inspired less than angelic thoughts. She was clearly frightened.

"Please sit down, signorina . . ."

"Stella Lasorella."

Stella! The girl about whom Fazio was trying to dig up information at that very moment!

"The medical student?" he asked.

Face already flushed with emotion, she turned fiery red all over.

40

"I guess you already know," she said, eyes downcast.

She suddenly started crying.

Montalbano got up, went and locked the door, grabbed the bottle of water that was atop the filing cabinet, filled a glass, handed it to her, and went and sat back down. She avidly drank half of it.

"Can I put this on the desk?"

"Of course."

"I'm . . . I'm sorry about my . . ."

"No problem. We can wait till you feel ready to talk."

The girl took a handkerchief from the pocket of her jeans, wiped her eyes, and blew her nose. Then she began.

"I heard on television last night . . . that some blond hair was found in the bed . . . Is that true?"

She hadn't mentioned any names.

"Yes."

"I've come here to tell you that it's not mine. I decided on my own to come here so that . . . to avoid . . . it's not my hair. You can conduct all the tests you want."

"So it wasn't you who slept with Barletta his last night."

"No."

Decisive, assured, looking him straight in the eyes.

41

"When was the last time you were at that house?"

"I went there only once. He wanted our first encounter to take place there. I never went back after that, also because it was already summer and he didn't want to risk any surprise visits from his son or daughter, both of whom had keys."

"Speaking of keys, did Barletta give you a set?"

"No."

"So where did your meetings with him take place?"

"At his place in town. It was easier that way."

"Explain what you mean."

"I live with my parents in the same building as Barletta. Which he owns. We rent a place on the third floor, he's on the second. When he would want me, he would arrange the doormat a certain way outside his door. When I saw this, I would do what I had to do at home, then would go downstairs to his place as soon as my parents fell asleep."

"They never suspected anything?"

"No, never! And I'm terrified at the thought that they might . . . Can you do anything to make sure my name doesn't . . ."

"I'll do what I can. But can you prove to me that you weren't at Barletta's beach house the other night?"

"I think so."

"Tell me how."

"I had a date with Giulio, my boyfriend, at nine o'clock that evening. We went first to eat pizza with a couple of friends, Antonio Burgio and Paola Nicotra, who can testify to this—I'll give you their addresses and phone numbers. Then the four of us went to the movies and came out after midnight. Since none of us was tired, we went to a discotheque. When I got home it was three o'clock. Is that enough?"

"Do you have a car?"

"No."

"Then I think that's enough."

The girl heaved a sigh of relief.

"There's one last question I'd like to ask you," said Montalbano, not taking his eyes off her. "Do you love your boyfriend?"

The question took the girl by surprise. Her face turned a hot red.

"Yes."

"Then, why?"

It was as if he'd clubbed her over the head.

The girl was transformed. She started trembling all over, tried to speak but couldn't, pressed her clenched fists hard against her cheeks.

Large beads of sweat started to appear on her forehead. Montalbano got worried that she might get hysterical.

Then the girl began to talk, keeping her teeth clenched and her voice low and muffled.

"Will you believe me if I tell you that when I

43

heard he'd been killed I started jumping for joy? In my mind I thanked the killer for giving me back my freedom."

She was now trembling even worse than before.

Montalbano got up, went over to the girl, made her drink the rest of the water in the glass, practically forcing her clenched jaw open, then sat down in the chair beside her and began very lightly stroking her forehead, brushing the hair away from it.

She began to relax her goggled eyes, letting the eyelids slowly droop and finally close.

Then, heaving another deep sigh, she took Montalbano's wrists, turned them over, and pressed the palms of his hands over her cheeks, as if he were caressing them. Then she released them.

"Thank you," she said.

The inspector realized the crisis was over. And Stella started talking again in a normal voice:

"Four months ago my father was fired by the company he worked for. The unemployment payments he received were not enough to allow me to stay at the University of Palermo. So, without saying anything to my mother or me, he went to talk to Barletta, to ask him if he could defer the rent payments for a while. He was hoping to find another job in the meantime. But Barletta, as you might expect, refused. In fact he told him he would throw us out if he didn't pay on time. Papa was desperate and told us the whole story. Then one evening I ran into Barletta on the stairs and he stopped me. And made me a proposal, which you can imagine. In effect he would pay me the equivalent of the rent, which I would give to my father, and then Papa, without knowing anything, would give it back to Barletta."

"And how did you explain to your father where you got the money?"

"I said I'd won a scholarship. After losing his job my dad wasn't really all there and so he didn't ask many questions. And my mother's just a poor woman who . . . Then, luckily, my father found a new job. But Barletta wanted to continue."

"How could he make you?"

"He blackmailed me."

"How?"

"He'd secretly taken photos with his cell phone as I . . . And he showed them to me and threatened to send them to my parents and boy-friend if I didn't . . . He said I had to be at his beck and call until he no longer wanted me. Over the past month I managed not to run into him. But I couldn't sleep at night, for fear he would make good on his threat."

She looked up at the inspector and said by way of conclusion:

"I would spit on his corpse if I could."

Montalbano laid his hand over her mouth,

preventing her from saying any more. He stood up and held out his hand, which she shook, confused.

"You can go now," he said.

Stella quickly leaned over and kissed the hand she was still holding in her own.

As soon as the girl was gone, he rang Catarella.

"Get me Fazio on his cell and—"

"Beckin' yer partin, Chief, but why do ya wan' me t'call 'im on 'is sillphone?"

How dare he question an order?

"Cat, don't gimme any shit, just put him on when you get him."

"Whate'er ya say, Chief."

A minute later the phone rang.

"Fazio here, Chief. What is it?"

"What are you doing right now?"

"I'm checking my notes in my—"

"Drop everything and come to my office."

He barely had time to set the phone down when Fazio appeared in the doorway. Montalbano looked at him in astonishment. What, did he fly there? Or was his matter beamed there through space?

"Where were you?"

"In my office, Chief. I got back about five minutes ago, but since Catarella told me you were busy . . . Why'd you call me on my cell, anyway?"

"No reason . . . I just felt suddenly like talking to you on your cell phone, okay? Have you got a problem with that?" said the inspector, incensed.

Fazio looked at him as if he'd gone completely insane.

"Hey, you're the boss."

Montalbano decided to change subject.

"You know who was just here with me?"

"No, sir."

"Stella."

Fazio's eyes opened wide.

"The same girl who—"

"The same girl."

And he told Fazio everything. When he was done, he asked:

"What were you able to find out about her?"

"Her last name, in the meantime."

"How did you do that?"

"There's an organization in Vigàta that brings together local university students. There's only one female medical student, Stella Lasorella."

"Anything else?"

"Yes. Everyone says she's a good girl and a serious person. And she has a boyfriend whose name is Giulio Marchica."

"She seemed like a serious person to me too. Listen, has Tommaseo had seals put up at Barletta's place in town as well?"

"Yes."

"Who has the keys?"

"I do."

"Let's go have a look."

The apartment was spacious and fairly neat. A main entrance, living room, two large bedrooms with double beds, a study, kitchen, two bathrooms. In the study was a large black nineteenth-century desk.

The inspector went straight for it.

In the top drawer on the right he found twenty-odd yellow so-called business envelopes. On each was written a woman's name: Rita, Giulia, Rosalba.

He grabbed one at random and pulled out the ten or so photos that were inside. They all showed the same girl, naked, in obscene poses or in the act of having sex with Barletta.

"Do me a favor, Fazio, would you? Go into the kitchen and see if you can find a shopping bag of some sort."

Fazio returned with a plastic bag and Montalbano put all the yellow envelopes in it.

"Let's go. You take this stuff to the station. Keep trying to dig up information on the Barlettas, father and son. I'm going to go eat. We'll meet back up later."

4

He took his walk to the lighthouse at the end of the jetty more slowly than usual, one small step at a time—stopping to watch first an angler with a line and rod, then a fishing boat returning to shore—because at Enzo's he'd feasted on octopus *a strascinasale,* and it's well known that octopus, even when so very tender as this was, puts up a fierce struggle in the stomach before surrendering to digestion.

He sat down on the flat rock and let the sun warm him for some ten minutes or so. Then he fired up a cigarette. He wanted to clear his head of thoughts for a few minutes. But he didn't succeed. The brain is a big ball-busting machine that not only never stops, but forces you to think whatever it wants. In vain you try to recall the happy moments of your life: after less than five minutes your brain will force you to think about things you'd rather not remember.

He started tossing sea pebbles into a puddle of water between two rocks and then watching the concentric circles ripple.

After a few minutes of this, he decided his pause was over and went back to thinking about the murder of the ragioniere.

Certainly neither of Barletta's two children had

painted a nice portrait of their father. They said he had a nasty disposition and that in business matters he wasn't the most sensitive man in the world.

But the brushstrokes young Stella had added to the portrait had further darkened the picture. Not only was Barletta unscrupulous in business, but he was a man capable of taking advantage of a young woman in trouble and even blackmailing her so he could keep sleeping with her.

In plain words, the number of people motivated by hatred for him probably reached three figures.

In even plainer words, the case was shaping up to be a tremendous pain in the ass. There would be hundreds of leads to follow, and they would all prove wrong in the end.

And it wasn't as if he was itching to dive headlong into the investigation.

Because it was one thing to send the killer of a good man to jail, and it was something else entirely to put away someone who had killed a stinking scoundrel.

The other Montalbano, the one who lurked inside him, ready to pop up at the slightest excuse, immediately came forward.

"Congratulations, Salvo. You really have a lofty sense of justice! Talk about double standards!"

"You know that's just the way I am."

"Then I guess you weren't made right!"

"No, I certainly wasn't! And I don't know what to do about it. If an honest man resolves to kill some guy who has driven him to despair, I tend to take his side."

"And so, with that kind of thinking, you end up justifying those who take justice into their own hands."

"Not on your life! I'm only saying that when I have to put the handcuffs on a person like that, a person who rebels against his oppressor, I feel nothing but 'comprassion'—as Catarella would say. And now that's enough, because I have to go back to the office."

He took his time returning to the office as well, since there were still a few octopi that hadn't yet surrendered.

"Is Fazio here?" he asked as he entered the station.

" 'E's onna premisses, Chief."

"Tell him to come to my office."

The moment he set foot in his office, he noticed that the teetering stack of papers had disappeared from his desktop. Was it possible? Had a miracle occurred? Had the Good Lord ordered his angels to make all bureaucratic memos disappear from the face of the earth?

Fazio came in with the plastic bag in hand.

"Oh, Chief, I removed the papers myself."

"Why?"

"They'd fallen on the floor. I put them in the closet."

What a disappointment. For a moment, the inspector had hoped the Supreme Being had had a bout of good sense . . . Fazio, meanwhile, emptied the bag onto the desk.

"We can have a look at these later," said Montalbano, gathering up the yellow envelopes with the pictures of the girls inside and putting them in the middle drawer.

"I found something out about Barletta," Fazio said as he was sitting down.

"Just one thing?"

"I haven't had much time yet, Chief. But what I did find out seems pretty important to me."

"And what's that?"

"Barletta was a loan shark."

"Are you sure?"

"Absolutely. Do you remember that great big clothing warehouse near the monument to the fallen that went bankrupt?"

"Sure, the Brancato warehouse."

"That's the one. The bankruptcy was Barletta's handiwork. He ate up Brancato's capital with four hundred percent interest rates. And he snatched up the warehouse while he was at it. They also told me Brancato wasn't his only victim. Apparently another businessman committed suicide because of Barletta."

That was all they needed. Not only was Barletta

an unscrupulous businessman, a womanizer, and a blackmailer, he was also a loan shark!

"Try to find out more."

"Okay."

"Do you realize that with this wonderful news you've just brought me, half the people in town could now be considered suspects?"

"You're right, Chief, but that's just the way it is. Where should we start, in your opinion?"

Good question. The inspector hadn't the slightest idea. Then the only thing possible came to mind.

"Is Inspector Augello around?"

"Yessir."

"Go and get him, would you?"

While Fazio was out, Montalbano took the yellow envelopes out of the drawer and set them down on the desk.

"Hello," said Mimì Augello, coming in with Fazio behind him.

"Hi, have a seat."

Grabbing an envelope at random, the inspector pulled out a photo and looked at it.

A naked young woman lay on a bed with her legs raised and spread as far as they would go.

He showed it to Mimì.

"You like the merchandise, sir?" he asked in the tone of a street peddler.

"I'll say!" exclaimed Mimì.

"Good. Then you and Fazio will stay here and

examine these photos one by one. See if you can manage to recognize any of the girls. I'm going to Montelusa and will be back in about an hour and a half at the latest."

He got up.

"Are you going to see the commissioner?" asked Mimì.

"Not a chance! No, I'm going to see Pasquano."

The traffic seemed snakebitten, convulsive and chaotic, and the inspector, who didn't like to drive, spent thirty minutes sweating more profusely than if he were in a sauna.

He pulled up in front of the institute, but before getting out of the car, he smoked a cigarette to settle his nerves and dry off a little.

Then he made up his mind and went inside.

"Is the doctor in?" he asked the porter, whom he knew.

"He's in his office."

"What kind of mood is he in?"

"The usual."

Which meant that one had to proceed with caution.

He knocked lightly at the door. No answer. He knocked a little harder. Nothing. And so he opened the door and went in.

He was greeted by a loud yell.

"You are the only person I know who will enter a room even if no one says to come in! And you are the only person I know liable to come and bust a good man's chops when he is hard at work!"

"Does your work involve principally eating the four cannoli you have in front of you?"

Pasquano chuckled.

"They're very good, you know. Would you like one?"

Montalbano accepted. It was truly good, and he savored it.

"Now that you've satisfied your gluttony—which no doubt stems from your growing senility—do you mind telling me what the hell you want?"

Always so courteous and kind, the doctor.

"Can't you guess?"

"I can. But I enjoy hearing you ask me things."

Montalbano put on a very serious, concerned face.

"I don't know whether . . ."

"Go on, go on."

"Would you do me a favor and lend me fifty thousand euros? I'm badly in need."

Pasquano did a double take.

"Are you serious?"

"No, but since you like to hear me ask for things, I thought I would lay it on thick."

Pasquano started laughing.

"You know I fell for it? You're a good actor! Is that how you screw all the poor bastards who fall into your hands? My compliments. So, do you want to know about Ragioniere Barletta?"

"If you would be so kind."

"My, my, such fancy language! But, just to make conversation and pass the time, tell me: How, according to your acute intelligence, do you think he was killed?"

"By a gunshot to the base of the skull."

Pasquano looked at him with an air of commiseration and shook his head repeatedly.

"How old are you?"

"Fifty-eight."

"Then that doesn't explain the deterioration of your brain, which must be premature. You're too old to continue this job. Why don't you retire? I've already told you a dozen times. Take the advice of a friend. It would be to your advantage, and it would be to mine, too, because I wouldn't have you here every other day busting my balls."

"Doctor, between all your poker games and autopsies, have you ever stopped to think that you're one year older than me?"

"Of course, my friend, but age has nothing to do with it! *My* head works just fine!"

"Which one?"

Pasquano absorbed the blow in his own way. He threw his head back and started laughing to the point of tears. Then he caught hold of himself.

"But can you explain to me how, with all your experience, you didn't notice that there was—"

"—not much blood spilt for the kind of wound it was?"

"There you go!"

"Well, I did notice, as you can see."

"And, if you noticed, why didn't you do the math? Why didn't you draw the obvious conclusion?"

"Conclusions are your domain, Doctor, and I always respect assigned roles."

"You? Don't make me laugh! Come on, out with your questions."

"Why did you want Forensics to examine the remains of the coffee?"

"See? Even you figured that one out."

"Was he already dead when he was shot?"

"Quite."

"Was he poisoned?"

"Quite."

"But why did the killer first poison him and then shoot him?"

"That's not my job to find out, but yours. All the same, I'll give you a little hint, like they do on TV game shows: Whoever said it was the same person?"

"What time did he die?"

"That's the first intelligent question you've asked," said Pasquano. "No later than six a.m."

"What kind of poison?"

"I can see that, however sporadically, your brain still functions. I'll spare you the scientific name and tell you only that it produces immediate paralysis followed by sudden death."

"Let me get a handle on that."

"Okay. But how long will that take? Because, if it's gonna be long, I've got stuff to do."

"Just a few more questions and you can eat the last cannolo."

"No, not 'a few' more questions. That's too vague. Let's say two questions."

"Okay. One: Is it possible the paralysis brought on by the poison kept Barletta sitting up in his chair as if he was still alive?"

"Quite possible."

"Had he had sexual relations?"

"Barletta didn't like water and didn't wash very often. Yessirree, he had indeed had sexual relations."

"Can you tell me whether—"

"Time's up. I won't see you to the door; you know the way out."

"Can you give me half a cannolo?"

"Not even if you get down and your knees and beg."

When he got back to the office, Pitrotta, a vice squad officer, was with Fazio and Augello.

"We asked for help," said Mimì.

"You were right. Any results?"

"We've identified two girls. I recognized one, Pitrotta the other."

Montalbano looked inquisitively at the vice officer, who picked up an envelope with the name *Janicka* on it and handed it to him. Montalbano didn't open it.

"In the usual poses?"

"In the usual poses."

"Who is she?"

"A Slavic girl, nineteen years old," said the vice officer. "We arrested her three months ago because she had no papers. I think she was repatriated."

"Try to confirm and then get back to me. Thanks, Pitrotta."

The officer said good-bye and left.

"And who's your girl?" Montalbano asked Mimì.

"This one," Augello replied, handing him an envelope with the name *Stefania* on it.

"Which whorehouse did you meet her in?"

Augello looked over at Fazio, who immediately got the message.

"Excuse me, I'll be back in five minutes," said Fazio, getting up hastily and going out.

"So?"

"I didn't meet her in a brothel, but at some friends' place. She's twenty-one years old and works as a salesgirl in a perfume shop."

"And she prostitutes herself?"

"Salvo, you gotta believe me: When you talk about women, you're a hundred years behind the times."

"Then explain to me what kind of woman lets herself be photographed while she's—"

"She's someone who's okay with it if she feels like it."

"But she gets paid for it."

"Not always. Don't start categorizing."

"Did you make it with her?"

"I appreciate the delicacy with which you pose the question. I could have, but I decided not to."

"Why?"

"I didn't trust her."

"Explain."

"She seemed like the clinging type, you know what I mean? The type liable to ring you at home . . . to write you notes . . . very dangerous notes. I keep away from women like that."

"You prefer the hit-and-run types?"

"Listen, we're not here to discuss my tastes in women. Do you want me to summon the girl here?"

"No. You go and talk to her yourself, since you already know her."

"What do you want to know?"

"Everything. How they started, how long it lasted, where they used to meet, why the relationship ended, what kind of man Barletta was, what kind of presents he gave her . . ."

"Okay."

"Do you need the photos?"

"No," said Mimì, handing him the envelope.

Montalbano put it back with the others. What a fine collection Barletta had built up! Fazio returned.

"Can I go?" asked Augello.

"Just five more minutes. Fazio, have a seat. Pasquano told me that Barletta wasn't killed by a gunshot."

Fazio jumped out of his chair.

"Are you kidding me?"

"No."

"So how'd he die?"

"Poisoned. Somebody spiked his coffee."

"Mind telling me what you two are talking about?" asked Augello, who wasn't well-informed about Barletta's death.

Montalbano brought him up to speed.

"So there were two killers?" Augello asked when he'd finished.

"So it would seem."

"But what need was there to shoot him after he was already dead?"

"I know a possible explanation."

"What?"

"The two killers acted without knowledge of each other's actions. The first one kills him with poison, and—"

"Wait a second," Fazio cut in. "He was drinking

61

his coffee when he died—we know that because he knocked the cup over. So why didn't the body fall to the floor?"

"But how do you know they didn't fire the shot when he was already on the ground?"

"No, Inspector Augello, they couldn't have. The bullet's trajectory speaks loud and clear. It entered at the base of the skull, came out through his face, and ended up in the wall in front of him."

"He died sitting up and stayed that way," said Montalbano, to clarify. "Pasquano told me this was possible because the poison used paralyzes its victims. Turns them stiff as statues. Which can mean only one thing."

"What?" Mimì and Fazio asked in chorus.

"That the second person, the one who shot him, thought he was alive."

Fazio gave him a puzzled look.

"But that's hard to believe!" was Mimì's comment.

"That's why, I repeat, we are dealing with two people acting without each other's knowledge."

"I'm starting to have an inkling," said Fazio.

"Let's hear it."

"On the rack over the kitchen sink there was a demitasse, a saucer, and a little spoon, all washed and rinsed. Which means that the killer had coffee with Barletta, slipped the poison into his cup when he wasn't looking, and when he was sure he was dead, he carefully washed the things he'd touched, and then calmly left, closing the door behind him. But my conclusion is this: that the killer was not a he but a she, the same woman who spent the night with him. Poisoning, after all, is a favorite female way of killing."

"That's no longer the case," said Montalbano. "Ever since Hedda Gabler, women have been using guns."

"Who's this Grabber?" asked Mimì.

Montalbano felt like screwing around.

"Some Nordic dame who shot herself. The case was written about by a famous nineteenth-century criminologist named Ibsen."

"I think I remember that Ibsen was somebody who wrote stuff for the theatre," said Mimì.

"Very good, Mimì. The Ibsen I'm talking about was his twin brother."

"It used to be that when women wanted to kill themselves, they either took poison or threw themselves out the window," Fazio commented.

"The good old days!" Montalbano exclaimed. "At any rate, Fazio's reconstruction is plausible."

5

"The total implausibility begins the moment a second person comes in to kill Barletta," Mimì continued.

"Explain."

"Pasquano said he was killed no later than six a.m., right?"

"Right."

"Fazio's reconstruction is convincing. But before we go any further, I'd like to make one thing clear. Which is that Barletta and the woman he spent the night with had to have gotten out of bed no later than around five-thirty in the morning. Otherwise six o'clock as the time of death makes no sense. So the two get dressed and go down to the kitchen. The man makes coffee for both of them and dies from poisoning. Now my question is this: Why did they get up so early? According to what his son told us, Barletta had been planning to stay at home all day. There was no need for him to get up early. That probably means, therefore, that the woman had an engagement that prevented her from staying any longer with him. Does that make sense?"

"Go on," said the inspector, taking interest.

"Therefore the woman who was with him

must not be just any old prostitute, but a nonprofessional, a woman with commitments relating to family or work."

"I don't agree," said Fazio.

"Why not?"

"Maybe Barletta was afraid his son Arturo would come earlier than planned and didn't want him to see the woman there," Fazio explained.

"That's also possible," Augello admitted. "But we're left with the inexplicable fact that as soon as the woman leaves, after Barletta has died, the other killer comes in right after her. Which means: two people decide to kill the same person on the same day and at almost the same time of day. That's what doesn't make sense to me."

"Why did you say 'right after her'? Pasquano didn't tell me exactly when the gunshot was fired," said the inspector.

"But if there was blood around the body, it means he was shot right after he died! Maybe fifteen minutes later, but no more! Otherwise there wouldn't have been even a single drop of blood!"

"You're exaggerating, Mimì. But, at any rate, you're also right: The two murders, so to speak, took place during a span of time between five and eight a.m., when Arturo arrived."

"So, to conclude, we need to look for two killers who acted within a short time of each other," said Fazio.

"We have to make the effort for two, but if we catch both, they'll become one person in the eyes of the law."

"What do you mean?"

"Because the lawyer will say that his client was perfectly aware that Barletta was already dead, but that he shot him anyway, out of spite. And the guy'll get off with a conviction for violation of a corpse."

"Yes, but he technically remains a killer. His intention was to kill."

"You can't try a person for his intentions alone," said Montalbano, cutting short the discussion.

He felt suddenly tired. Maybe Pasquano was right.

"Listen, let's talk about this tomorrow morning with clearer heads."

It was a lovely evening. And so Montalbano decided, when he was still in the car, that he would set the table out on the veranda.

The first thing he did when he got home was to open the French door. He noticed at once that on the table outside were two pieces of paper weighted down by two rocks. The first was a message written on a sheet of notebook paper, which read:

I am truly grateful.

It wasn't signed. The handwriting was confident

66

and personal, like that of someone accustomed to using a pen.

The second piece of paper was the receipt from a bookbinder with the name *Inspector Salvo Montalbano* on it. The vagabond must have found it in a pocket of the brown suit.

The telephone rang. It was Livia.

"Think you can make it to Palermo to pick me up? My plane lands at noon."

He weighed his options. He decided he would drop in at the station to postpone his meeting with Augello and Fazio until the afternoon.

"I can make it."

"Listen, did you do what I asked you to do?"

"What?"

"To take those shirts, shoes, and a suit to—"

"Yes, I did. The poor guy even left me a note of thanks."

"What a strange person! I'm dying of curiosity to meet him."

Good! If Montalbano got too wrapped up in the investigation, Livia could spend time with the tramp, which might keep her from busting his chops.

He had a leaden sleep, deep inside a dark well, and when he woke up, it was raining buckets outside.

So, what was the weather up to? One good day and one bad day in alternation?

The fact was that the season was taking too long to end, he thought.

Then he suddenly remembered that he'd promised Livia he would come and get her at the airport.

No. He really didn't feel like driving at least two and a half hours in heavy rain.

He looked at his watch. Eight o'clock. How had he woken up so late? But surely Livia was still at home in Boccadasse.

He rang her.

"Who's this?" Livia asked with a note of alarm.

He didn't feel like telling her the truth, so he made up a lie on the spot.

"Listen, I just got a call from the commissioner, who wants to see me this morning at eleven. So I won't be able to come to get you. You can take the bus to Montelusa, which leaves directly from the airport."

"We're off to a good start!" said Livia.

"So, what's the plan?"

"What do you think? When I get to Montelusa I'll have a cab take me to your office."

She hung up.

Before going out, he left a note for Adelina on the kitchen table.

Livia's coming today and will be here for three days.

It was more than certain that the housekeeper would not show up during that time.

• • •

The road into Vigàta was completely clogged, with barely a millimeter of distance between one car and the next, and the average speed about a centimeter a minute.

It was past nine-thirty by the time he got to the station. He parked, got out of the car, and cursed the saints passionately for ten minutes straight to get the agitation out of his system. Then he went in.

"Ahh, Chief, Chief! Isspecter Augello's wit' Fazio in espectancy o' yiz."

"And I'm in arrivancy."

Augello and Fazio were standing outside the door to his office, talking. He showed them in and sat them down.

"Pitrotta came by my office," Fazio began, "and told me that it turns out the Slavic girl, whose name I can't remember, is probably no longer in Italy. It's possible she didn't go back to her country of origin but merely moved to another town, though that's hard to confirm."

"Yesterday evening," said Mimì, "I managed to talk to Stefania Interdonato, just as she was closing her perfume shop. Since she had no engagements, I invited her out to a restaurant."

"And what did you tell Beba?"

"That you kept me here late."

"How late?" Montalbano asked, alarmed.

For all he knew, the guy was likely to have

spent the night with the girl. He didn't like providing alibis for Mimì's infidelities to Beba.

"Don't worry, just till ten."

"And what did she tell you?"

"I'll proceed in orderly fashion. Actually, no, before I forget, she begged me in tears to give her the photographs of her. If possible, I'd like to—"

"We'll see about that later. Now talk."

"They met one day when Barletta came into her shop with a beautiful girl and bought her a fancy perfume. He never once took his eyes off Stefania. That same evening, at closing time, he was there, waiting for her, in front of the store, and he invited her out to dinner. She refused. But the second time, she accepted. Barletta was brilliant, a big talker, gallant, and very polite. A bit old-fashioned, and Stefania, in the end, was won over. That's how it started."

"Where would he take her?"

"To his beach house."

"Stefania would meet him there?"

"No, she doesn't have a car. He would take her there himself."

"How long did this last?"

"Four months."

"Did he give her presents?"

"Yes."

"Money?"

"Just once, he gave her ten thousand euros because she had a large payment due. At any rate, the stuff he gave her was always pretty valuable: rings, bracelets . . ."

So, sometimes he paid, and sometimes he blackmailed.

"Who broke off the relationship?"

"He did, of course. Imagine Stefania ever leaving him!"

"What did he say to her?"

"He didn't say anything. He just neglected to come and pick her up one evening at the perfumery. And she never saw him again after that. She sat tight for a few days, but then she went on the warpath."

"In what sense?"

"Didn't I tell you what the girl was like? She never gives up. She started writing to him and calling him up, to no avail. But then she got a good idea."

"She went to see him," said Montalbano.

"Bravo! Right on the money! Since she knew that Barletta spent every Saturday night at his beach house, she borrowed a friend's car and went there. At one o'clock in the morning, no less!"

"What did she do?"

"The shutters were all closed, and it was dark inside, but there were two cars parked outside the house, Barletta's and another. Therefore the guy was home, with company. To get him to open the door, she started knocking wildly, kicking the door and throwing rocks at it, until a woman finally came out. Just in her panties, without even a bra on. And she jumped on poor Stefania like a rabid dog, hitting her with a big stick. Stefania hadn't expected anything like that and was luckily able to get back in her car and drive away. She said the woman was bent on killing her."

"The woman must have been interrupted during the best part," Fazio commented.

"That's what Stefania thought, too, until she heard the woman, who was screaming obscenities at her—things like *whore, slut, cunt*—until she heard her say: 'You leave my father alone or I'll break your head!' It was his daughter. Barletta had sent her down to get rid of Stefania."

Montalbano chuckled.

"What's so funny?" asked Augello.

"Signora Giovanna, the daughter in question, assured Fazio and me, with great dignity, that she never involved herself in any way in her father's amorous adventures. If that was her way of not getting involved . . ."

"Giovanna told us that it was Arturo who quarreled with his father because he thought he spent too much on his women," Fazio confirmed.

"I wonder why, when I asked her for the names of some of the women Barletta frequented, she didn't mention Stefania?" Montalbano asked. "She did nearly bludgeon her to death, after all!"

"Maybe that's why," said Augello.

"Tell me something, Mimì. Do you know whether the slimeball Barletta took those pictures of her with her consent or not?"

"She swore to me she never gave her consent and didn't even know they existed. And having seen them myself, I believe her. Have you looked at them?"

"No, I haven't wanted to," Montalbano replied. "I don't know about you, but they make me uncomfortable."

Mimì resumed speaking:

"They're clearly photos taken on the sly while the girl was in action, so to speak. It was merely a stroke of luck that you can clearly see Stefania's face in one of them."

Montalbano opened the drawer, searched through the yellow envelopes, grabbed the one marked *Stefania*, and handed it to Augello.

"Give it back to her."

"Excuse me, Chief," Fazio intervened, "but aren't we supposed to be making these photos available to the prosecutor?"

"Have you lost your mind?"

"I'm sorry, Chief, but it would only—"

"Do you realize what could happen? Giving two hundred photographs of naked women in imaginative states of coition, as he might say, to Tommaseo? The guy's so sex starved he might never recover! And if he does recover, he'll institute a nationwide search for the girls so he can call them all into his office, where he'll have them all strip to verify their identities!"

"Chief, I think we should turn them over to him anyway," Fazio insisted.

"Ah, so now you've become a stickler for procedure? Okay, then it only means that instead of twenty envelopes, Tommaseo will get eighteen. At any rate, he doesn't know how many Barletta had in his desk. All right?"

"All right," said a resigned Fazio. "But why eighteen envelopes? Shouldn't there be nineteen?"

"Eighteen."

"I'm sorry, Chief, but twenty minus one makes nineteen."

Without answering, Montalbano opened the drawer again, grabbed all the envelopes, laid them out on the desk, looked for the one with Stella's name on it, then put it in his jacket pocket right before Fazio's astonished eyes.

Then he started counting them out loud.

"See? There's only eighteen," he said in conclusion.

Then he stuffed them all back in the drawer.

"And now let's resume yesterday's discussion."

"I thought the whole thing over last night," Fazio said after a pause, "and the only explanation I could come up with was that it was all a coincidence."

"Oh, come on!" Augello reacted. "Two people killing the same man at almost the same time!"

"I thought the same thing myself," said Montalbano. "And I came up with a hypothesis that might perhaps explain the quasi simultaneity."

"And what would that be?" asked Mimì.

"There was something they wanted to prevent Barletta from doing that same morning."

"I don't understand," said Fazio.

"I'll explain it myself," said Augello. "Our boss is conjecturing that the two killers wanted to prevent Barletta from carrying out something he had resolved to do that morning."

"But what?" said Fazio. "Don't forget it was Sunday! And on Sunday all the stores and offices are closed!"

"And anyway," said Mimì, "how did the two killers come to learn of Barletta's intentions?"

"He may have talked about it the day before with the girl who spent the night with him," the inspector replied.

"But in that case there would be only one killer: her!" Augello objected.

"And what reason could the girl have had for preventing him from doing what he had in mind to do?" Fazio pressed.

Montalbano surrendered. He threw up his hands.

"Calm down! It was only a conjecture!"

They all fell silent.

"The truth is," the inspector said after a few moments, "that we don't know where to begin."

Then he got an idea.

"Do you have Arturo Barletta's number?" he asked Fazio.

"Yessir."

"Ring him from here and then pass me the phone."

Fazio dialed the number, said hello, and then handed the receiver to Montalbano, who turned on the speakerphone.

"Montalbano here, hello. Sorry to bother you, but I need a clarification and some information."

"Whatever I can do to help."

"Thank you. If I remember correctly, you phoned your father Saturday evening and learned that he planned to spend the night at his beach house. Is that correct?"

"Not exactly. It was Papa who called me."

"At any rate, you told him you would go out to see him the following morning."

"That's right."

"What time was it when you got to the house?"

"Eight o'clock sharp."

"Are you sure you had to use the key to open the door?"

"Absolutely sure."

"Therefore whoever killed him had a set of keys?"

"But, Inspector, I already discussed this with you and—"

"Not with me, you didn't. You talked about it with the TV newsman."

"I'm sorry, I got confused. Anyway, I mentioned the possibility that there may be sets of keys that my father gave out to one of his girl—"

"Did your father spend every Saturday night at the beach house?"

"Well, yes."

"Then why, based on your testimony, did he tell you that on that Saturday he was going there with a specific purpose, which was to tidy up the house? Don't you think that's a bit of rather superfluous information?"

"Now that you mention it . . ."

"During that phone call, did he mention anything specific he planned to do the following morning, on Sunday?"

"But we just said what he planned to do! He went there to tidy—"

"—up the house, agreed. But didn't he mention anything else he had to do?"

"Absolutely not. At least not with me. Maybe . . ."

"Maybe what?"

"Maybe he mentioned something to Giovanna."

"Thank you, Signor Barletta."

He hung up and handed the phone back to Fazio.

"Now call Signora Giovanna for me."

Fazio repeated the operation.

"Montalbano here. Good morning, signora. Is this a bad time?"

"Not at all."

"I need some information. Did you phone your father on the Saturday before he died?"

"Of course, I called him every day."

"Did he tell you he would be spending the night at his beach house?"

"Yes."

"Did he tell you he would also be staying Sunday?"

"Yes."

"Did he tell you why?"

"No, but he often stayed there Sundays as well. He would spend the weekend there."

"Did he mention anything he had to do on Sunday morning?"

"Let me think about that for a moment."

She thought about it briefly and then said:

"Hello? No, I don't think so."

"But you're not sure?"

"Absolutely sure, no. But it was a . . . how shall I say? . . . a routine sort of conversation, of no consequence whatsoever . . . I didn't attach any particular importance to what he was saying . . ."

"I see."

"But maybe . . ."

"Maybe?"

"Maybe you should ask my brother."

"Thank you, signora. Have a good day."

6

"So, round and round we go, only to end up back where we started," said the inspector. "As far as we know, he didn't talk to his children about what he had to do. And that shoots holes in my hypothesis, which no longer holds water."

"Not necessarily," Fazio objected. "It's also possible he simply didn't want to tell his children."

"Or," said Augello, "he got a phone call late that evening, when he was already at the house, and the woman who was with him overheard."

"That doesn't hold up," said the inspector.

"Why not?"

"Because in that case there should only have been one killer. You said it yourself just now. And there's something else to consider: that the woman who was with him that night was already intending to kill him, since she already had the poison, which is not the sort of thing women are in the habit of carrying around in their purses."

"True," said a disconsolate Fazio.

"So the main problem becomes finding out who this woman is."

"Easier said than done!" said Augello.

"Fazio, I want you to get in touch with Stella Lasorella—but discreetly, mind you, without her parents finding out—and tell her to come and see me here around four o'clock. Mimì, you, on other hand, should put together a team and go and thoroughly search the beach house and his place in town."

"What are we looking for?"

"Beats me. Other photos, letters, whatever you can find that's marginally of interest."

He remembered Giovanna's words.

"See also if you can find a will."

"Ahh, Chief! 'At'd be the prassicutor Gommaseo!"

"Where? On the phone?"

"Yessir."

"Put him through."

"Dear Inspector, how are you?" Tommaseo opened.

"And how are you, good sir?"

"I don't want to waste your time, so I'll get straight to the point. I've received the report from Forensics. Apparently, they recovered, in the bed of that longtime widower, Signor Galletta—"

"Barletta."

"Between the rumpled sheets . . ."

The prosecutor's thoughts at that moment must have been a whirlwind of erotic images.

". . . three strands of female hair, long and blond! And then . . . and then . . ."

Montalbano imagined his superior with white beads of spittle foam forming at the corners of his mouth. The moment a murder investigation involved a woman, the man would lose his head.

"And what else?"

Tommaseo, who seemed for a moment as if he was dying of suffocation, managed to catch a breath.

"And . . . some . . . pubic hair . . . did you know?"

Maybe he had it there in front him, in a little plastic bag, and was contemplating the kinky strands spellbound. Montalbano decided to give him some rope.

"Are they the same color as her hair?"

"A little redder."

"So you think Barletta actually took two women to bed with him?"

"No, no! It's not uncommon for blonde women—natural blondes, that is—to have pubic hair . . ."

He started panting again.

". . . tending towards red."

"You know, my question wasn't as far-fetched as you may think, because the further we get in the investigation, the more we discover that Barletta was a tremendous womanizer."

"Really? What have you found out?"

"That he photographed all the women who went with him."

"How?"

"Naked, and in poses you can't imagine!"

"Oh, I can imagine, I can, and you must tell me!"

"And even while they were having intimate relations—full relations, oral, anal, and so on . . ."

"Ohmygod ohmygod ohmygod . . ."

"Are you all right, sir?"

"Wait just a second while I go and drink some water."

He returned moments later, but still quite agitated.

"But . . . you say . . . you *found* these photos?"

"Yes. There's about a hundred and eighty of them."

For a few moments all the inspector could hear over the line was Tommaseo's breathing, which sounded like that of a deep-sea diver whose tank had run out of oxygen.

"You must send them to me at once!" the prosecutor ordered him.

Montalbano decided to obey immediately. That way the guy would lose himself poring over the photos and stay out of his hair for a while.

He figured Livia wouldn't get to Vigàta before two-thirty. He glanced at his watch. It was already one o'clock.

Just to be safe, he rang Enzo and warned him that he would be coming late to eat with Livia.

And now, how was he going to make the time pass?

There was only one thing to do: sign a few

papers. Sighing, he got up, went over to the closet, opened it, grabbed a handful of files, set them down on the desk, sat back down, grabbed a pen, and started scribbling.

Just as he'd calculated, at half past two, Catarella informed him that his "ladygoilfrenn'" had arrived. Montalbano put the papers back in the closet and went out.

Livia was waiting for him outside his car. As he drew near, he noticed that she was a little thinner but also gave the impression of being a little younger.

They embraced and held each other tight. Their bodies understood one another in an instant, even though their brains often operated on different planes.

"Don't you have any luggage?"

"Yes. One suitcase. Catarella's already put it in the car for me."

"Shall we go?"

"Yes, I'm a little hungry."

"You can imagine me!"

To celebrate Livia's arrival, Enzo had done things up in grand fashion. Livia didn't know how to cook, that was clear, but she certainly knew how to eat.

When they'd finished, the inspector thought that a walk along the jetty would be a blessing, but with Livia there it wasn't going to work.

"Let's drive you home."

As soon as they there, Montalbano took the suitcase out of the car while Livia unlocked the front door with her own set of keys. Montalbano called to her, and she turned around. It had stopped raining.

"Look over at the hill, halfway up. See the hole near that large clump of sorghum? That's the entrance to the cave where our hobo lives."

He carried the suitcase into the bedroom and then asked:

"So, what's the plan?"

"Do you have to leave immediately?"

Montalbano looked at his watch.

"I guess I've got about an hour."

Without saying a word, Livia embraced him and pulled him down onto the bed.

"But what did you do?"

"What are you talking about?"

"I'm talking about this. And this . . . and this . . . and this . . ."

"Ah! Ah! You're tickling me! No, stop, please!"

"You have marvelous skin. And you're all . . . I don't know how to put it . . . you're all firmed up."

"I didn't tell you, but I've been going to a gym for the past six months. You should do the same, it would do you some good."

That was all he needed, a gym! Anyway, he had other things on his mind at that moment.

"Man oh man! Your body is so . . ."

"Do you like it?"

"I'll show you how much I like it!"

"But didn't you have to go back to work?"

"I can waste another half hour or so."

"What did you say? So with me it's time wasted?"

"You didn't hear right. I said: 'I can take another half hour or so.' "

"You said 'waste,' I heard you perfectly fine!"

"Okay, okay, I'm sorry, I used the wrong verb."

"Asshole."

"Listen, can we postpone the quarrel until this evening?"

It was past four when he got to the office.

"Ah, Chief! 'Ere's 'at young lady wit' 'er sister's name 'oo's waitin' f'yiz inna waitin' room."

"Show her into my office."

Stella Lasorella came in and looked around, pressing her lips together. She was even more frightened than the first time.

"Why did you . . ."

"Please sit down. And please don't worry. I called you in here first of all to tell you that I found the photos that Barletta secretly took of you."

Stella gave such a start in her chair that she risked falling. She turned bright red and hung her head and stared at the floor.

"Did you . . . look at them?"

"No."

"Then how do you know they're of me?"

Montalbano took the yellow envelope out of his jacket pocket and handed it to her.

"The envelope's got your name on it."

The girl opened it, took out a photo, and looked at it. Immediately she threw the envelope and photo back onto the desk and shot to her feet. She was deathly pale.

"Please . . . a bathroom."

Montalbano got up, grabbed her by the arm, led her down the hall, opened the bathroom door, pushed Stella inside, followed her in, and closed the door behind him. The girl propped herself against the wall with her hand and started vomiting into the toilet bowl, with Montalbano holding her head.

Then he took her over to the sink, turned on the water, splashed some around her mouth, and dried her face with his handkerchief.

"Do you feel up to going back into my office?"

He was talking to her in a familiar tone, as if to a . . . daughter.

She nodded her head yes. But as they came out of the restroom she seized the inspector's arm. She was having trouble standing, her legs giving out from under her. Once back in the office, he sat her down.

"Would you like some water?"

"No."

She swallowed and then frowned in disgust.

"I have this nasty taste . . ."

It occurred to Montalbano that he had a box of chocolates somewhere for reasons unknown even to him. He found it at the bottom of a drawer and gave it to her.

Stella took one, unwrapped it, and put it in her mouth.

Watching her movements, Montalbano felt sorry for her. She seemed like a little girl.

He put the photo back in the envelope and handed it to her.

"You can take these with you. I advise that you burn them."

The girl's face brightened.

"So no one will see them?"

"No one at all."

Stella sat there for a moment holding the envelope. She was thinking of something. Then, brusquely, she handed the envelope back to him.

"Could *you* burn them?"

"Of course."

He put the envelope back in his jacket pocket.

"Listen, I also called you in here to ask you something."

"You can ask me whatever you like."

"You told me you weren't with Barletta that night."

Stella got upset.

"I swear it's true! I wasn't at his house that night! I can prove it to you by—"

"I don't need any proof. I believe you. That wasn't my question. When was the last time you were with him?"

"A little over a month ago."

"Why did he let so much time go by?"

"Well, it went like this. The very same day my dad found a new job, I called Barletta and told him I couldn't see him anymore. But he said that it was better if we met in person. And he told me to come and see him at the usual hour."

Could that have been the phone call Giovanna overheard?

"Try and remember. When you made that phone call, was he the one who answered?"

"No, it was his daughter. She put him on right away."

"And what did you do?"

"I went there determined to put an end to it. But as soon as I started talking, he interrupted me and told me he had photographed me and would show those photos—which were explicit and compromising—to my parents if I didn't . . . What could I do? In the end he told me he would want me again soon and that if I didn't obey . . .

My nights became a living hell. I didn't know what to do. Should I accept going to bed with him again? Or should I cut things off, knowing he would take revenge by revealing the photos? I already told you that when he wanted me, he would . . ."

"Arrange the doormat a certain way, I remember."

"Every evening I would pass by his door with my heart racing, but I always found the doormat in its normal position. And it stayed that way for a month, until I learned he'd been killed."

"Why do you think he never called you again?"

Stella thought about this for a moment.

"I'm sure he met another woman he was more interested in."

"How can you be so sure?"

"Because Barletta was a maniac. He was obsessed. He couldn't go for a whole month without . . ."

"Do you have even a vague idea of who this last girl might be?"

"I don't think so . . ."

"Think it over before answering. In your last meetings with him, did you notice any kind of change in him?"

A furrow appeared in the middle of the girl's brow. She was leaning back in her chair and keeping her eyes closed. She sat there a long time in silence, then made up her mind to talk.

"As far as I can recall, he was the same. Odious, disgusting, and mean."

Stefania had spoken differently of him, however.

"Why mean? How did he treat you? Did he ever strike you?"

"No. But he treated me like some object to use up and throw away."

"But did he talk to you? What did he say?"

"He never talked to me."

"Not a single word?"

"Not in any proper sense. He would speak only to order me around. When I would get there he would already be naked, and he would say: 'Take your clothes off slowly.' He got the most pleasure in humiliating me. He would say things like: 'Turn around, get down on all fours, open your mouth.' He made me do horrible things, and he was never satisfied. He would say things like: 'You're basically worthless, you know.' Or: 'You were better last time.' And when he was done with me he would simply say: 'Get out of here.' Never a kind word."

She paused and then said:

"I'm convinced that, in the end, he didn't really like me physically."

"Then why did he keep on . . . ?"

"Because I think he found it terribly exciting to have me completely in his power."

And that went a long way towards explaining a character as complex as Barletta.

The inspector wrote down some numbers on a sheet of paper and stood up as he handed it to the girl.

"Here are the numbers to my office and my home. If you happen to remember anything strange in Barletta's behavior, or anything else— even the slightest thing, mind you—give me a call."

Later he got a call from Mimì Augello.

"We've just finished searching the house."

"Find anything?"

"Nothing of any importance. Now we're going to his place in town. I think that'll take a bit longer."

"Think you'll be there till nightfall?"

"Yes."

"Do me a favor, Mimì. If you find anything, ring me at home. I'll be going out to dinner with Livia around eight, but we'll definitely be back by ten."

He'd arranged with Livia to come and pick her up in Marinella at eight.

It was seven o'clock, but since he had nothing to do at the station other than sign those hated papers, he left to go home.

There was little traffic, and so by seven-twenty

he was opening his front door. Livia wasn't there. Perhaps she'd taken the bus from Montereale and gone into town to do some shopping. The return bus would pass at quarter to eight, so she would still be in time for their appointment.

He knew there was nothing in the fridge or oven. It was as sure as death that Adelina, out of spite over Livia's arrival, hadn't prepared anything to eat for that evening. He looked inside both just to pass the time, and indeed there was nothing but air.

He decided to take a leisurely shower. There was time, after all. Having done this, he changed all his clothes.

He looked at his watch. It was eight. He went to the door and looked outside to see if there was any sign of Livia coming down the road. Nothing. He went back in.

Maybe she'd missed the bus. The next one would pass at nine.

But why didn't she call? Did she think he was still at the office?

The best thing was to ring her. He dialed her cell phone number, but the usual obnoxious female voice came on, telling him the person he was trying to reach was unavailable.

Where the hell had she gone off to?

He rang the office.

"Yer orders, sah!"

"Listen, Catarella, has Livia by any chance come by there or called?"

"Nah, Chief, she din't come by or call, no ways."

"Well, if she does come by or call, tell her to ring me at home."

At quarter past eight he finally heard the front door open. Livia came in, out of breath.

"Sorry, I'm fifteen minutes late."

"Fifteen minutes? I've been waiting for you since seven-thirty!"

"Our appointment was for eight, so I'm only fifteen minutes late. If you want to come home half an hour early, that's your business. Seven-thirty and eight o'clock are not the same thing!"

"Where were you?"

"I went to see someone."

"Who?"

"Listen, don't you use that police-inspector tone of voice with me!"

"Tell me who you went to see!"

"I'm not going to tell you, okay? And don't insist!"

"As you wish. Come on, let's go eat."

"Where?"

"To Enzo's."

"Wait while I go and change my shoes. I got these ones all muddy."

As she went into the bedroom to change, Montalbano realized who the person was she'd gone to see. The hobo. She'd climbed up the hill to the cave and in the process had muddied her shoes.

"Okay, I'm ready," she said, coming out.

They went out in silence, drove in silence, and entered Enzo's trattoria in silence.

Not until they'd eaten a seafood antipasto to wake the dead did the inspector speak.

"So, tell me how your visit to the cave went."

7

She'd spent too many years at Montalbano's side to be surprised by his question.

"You figured it out from the shoes?"

"Yes."

"And that was why I told you. I wanted to see if you could do it, to see whether your policing abilities, at least, still functioned."

"What do mean, 'at least'? Are you implying that some of my other abilities don't function?"

"I'm not saying they don't function. All the same . . ."

Was she spoiling for a fight?

"Listen, Livia, you're trying to provoke me simply because you don't want to admit you gave yourself away. So knock it off with the barbs about my more or less functional abilities and tell me about your visit."

"Well, when I decided to go to the cave, I really didn't think I would find him there."

"Then why did you go?"

"To leave him a present."

"What kind of present?"

"Two new shirts of yours."

Montalbano felt his blood run cold.

"The ones Adelina bought me?"

"Yes. They were ghastly."

This was a genuine low blow of the kind that should be outlawed in the rules of marriage. Or quasi marriage, that is. She'd done it not out of generosity, but to make trouble between him and his housekeeper. So what was he going to tell Adelina now, when she discovered that the shirts were no longer in his armoire?

He certainly couldn't tell her that Livia had given them away, or things between the two women would end up in the gutter and he would suffer the consequences. In other words, it would be playing right into Livia's hands. Good thing he had two days to think of a good excuse. He remembered a little proverb he'd made up one time, which went as follows:

If Adelina gets mad, it means you eat bad.

For this reason, it was best to pretend it was nothing and not give Livia anything else to feel spiteful about.

"So tell me what you did."

"Well, I put them in a plastic bag and went to the cave. He was inside, sitting on a rickety chair, reading a book by the light of an oil lamp."

"What was the book?"

"I didn't get a chance to see the title on the cover. He got up, bowed to me, and told me to make myself comfortable in his chair while he put the book away in one of the cardboard boxes in the corner. Then he sat on the box. He didn't ask me what I was doing there. We just sat in silence for a spell."

"And then what?"

"I gave him the bag with the shirts. He thanked me, looked inside, and then asked me if I was your wife. Who knows how he'd managed to figure out . . ."

"He didn't figure anything out. In fact, you're not my wife."

"Well, aren't you witty tonight!"

"Come on, I was just kidding! He's an intelligent man. He must have wondered how it could be that, in the course of a few days, first a man and then a woman brought him clothing as gifts. And his answer must have been that the two visits were related, and so he asked you the most logical question."

"He seems like a cultured man."

"I got the same impression."

"He's polite and has perfect manners. And so . . ."

"And so?"

"You end up wanting to ask him why he lives that way."

"I don't. It would be improper."

"You think so?"

"Didn't he tell you anything about himself of his own accord?"

"Nothing about before."

"What do you mean?"

"He didn't tell me anything about his previous

life, from before he became an actual vagrant. Which I suppose he isn't really. The only thing you can really tell about him is that he's definitely not Sicilian. You can hear it in his accent. He said he came this way six years ago almost by chance, and that he liked it here and stayed. When he was talking I felt like laughing."

"Why?"

"He sounded like some rich tourist telling you why he'd decided to spend the rest of his days in Hawaii."

"Funny, I never noticed that before."

"He explained that when he first arrived six years ago, he'd set himself up in a district called . . . wait, I can't remember . . . the name had something to do with a dog . . . well, never mind, it's not important . . . But after a while he didn't like being there anymore, so he came to Scala dei Turchi . . . He discovered the cave only three months ago."

She paused a moment and cast a quick glance at Montalbano.

"You know what?"

"I'm no mind reader."

"But obnoxious, yes. If I tell you, will you get angry?"

"You let him seduce you among the cardboard boxes?"

"You are such a jerk! I'm not telling you anything else!"

"If you tell me I'll give you this crispy little calamari ring."

Livia laughed and continued.

"I invited him to lunch tomorrow."

Montalbano got worried. He was terrified not by the idea of the vagabond's presence, but by the prospect of Livia's cooking.

"And what did he say?"

"He refused, but with the utmost politeness."

"And this confirms that he's a very intelligent man."

"But I would like to get to know him better, to help him . . ."

"Did he tell you he needed help?"

"No."

"So then why do you want to help him?"

"Because I can feel that he wants—"

"He wants to be left alone, believe me. Listen: Since, like all women, you're extremely curious, you're just dying to know this man's secret."

"So you're saying it's only curiosity on my part?"

"I would say so, yes."

Livia resumed eating her second course and said no more.

When he got to the station the following morning, Mimì Augello was already there waiting for him.

He was unshaven, his clothes rumpled, eyes glazed, face sagging with fatigue.

100

"Why didn't you call me last night when you finished?"

"Because I didn't finish last night, but barely ten minutes ago. That is, we stopped because we were all dead tired. We're going to resume work this afternoon at four."

"How come you're not done searching—"

"Because the house has an attic full of old stuff, including hundreds of packets of letters and documents. I decided it was better to sift through all the papers there, instead of filling up our offices here with bags."

"Listen, come to think of it, did you find a will?"

"No. If he made one out, it may be among all those papers I haven't looked at yet."

"Have you found anything useful?"

"Maybe. Barletta engaged in a lot of activities in his life, always with an eye to making money, and so there's tons of contracts, notarized deeds, and documents of all kinds. It's a big pain in the ass."

"Any love letters?"

"No."

"Written messages?"

"No."

"Strange."

"Why?"

"You yourself told me that Stefania badgered him with phone calls and written messages . . . How come there are none to be found?"

"What makes you think he kept them?"

"Come on! A vain guy like that? So he kept the photos of the women but not their letters?"

"I repeat: We haven't finished looking at everything."

"Tell me meanwhile what you did find."

"These two letters."

Mimì took them out of his jacket pocket and laid them on the desk.

"I'll be seeing you. I'm going to get some sleep."

The two letters consisted of two sheets of paper without any envelope. The inspector read the first, which was handwritten. It was dated twenty days before. It read:

> Ever since I asked you for the loan I knew you would ignobly take advantage of the fact. I had no illusions. Your ruthless loan-sharking ways had been described to me by two of your victims. But I had no choice but to turn to you because the banks had cut off all my credit. And, as could have been expected, you managed in just two years to reduce me and my family to utter misery. Now I have nothing more to lose. Do you know what that means? A man who has nothing to lose can be dangerous. I bid you pleasant dreams, if you're capable.

At the bottom there was even a signature: *Riccardo Noto.*

So, they were finally starting to have something to work with. This was a concrete death threat.

The second letter was also handwritten, but it had no date and read:

A frend a mine warned me you was capable of anything but I din't believe it You aint a man but a piece of shit, a disgusting animal who's head should be squarshed one day some one's gonna kill you and when he does he'll rid the earth of one a the worse criminils an if some body don't do it I'll do it myself with no regrets and in fact itll be a pleasure You took everything I had an made my wife go crazy.

It wasn't signed.

This, too, was a death threat. Which, with the first, made two. Too much of a good thing! At any rate, searching Barletta's residences had been a good idea.

He called Fazio and gave him the two letters to read. When he was done, Fazio looked at him and said:

"This is our proof that he was loan-sharking."

"Do you know this Riccardo Noto?"

"The name rings a bell but I don't remember why."

"Well, when you do remember, let me know. And we have to find out who wrote the unsigned letter."

"The guy says his wife went crazy. If he's just saying it in a manner of speaking, it'll be hard to find out his name. But if his wife really did go crazy and was taken to an insane asylum, then the whole thing becomes a lot easier."

"But there aren't any more insane asylums!"

"There are still mental health care homes and treatment centers."

"Okay. Start looking right away."

Barely ten minutes had passed when Fazio reappeared in front of the inspector.

"Don't tell me it's already taken care of or I'll get pissed off!"

"No, Chief, I just wanted to tell you I remember what it was that I'd heard about Riccardo Noto, and I made a few phone calls to confirm. He died."

Montalbano gave a start in his chair.

"How'd he die?"

"Killed by a hit-and-run driver, about ten days ago."

"Have they found the driver?"

Fazio smiled.

"I was thinking the same thing when I heard. Namely, that Barletta, after Noto threatened him, decided to take him out of the picture."

"Whereas?"

"Whereas the hit-and-run driver has been identified and arrested by the carabinieri. And it turns out it was a woman who had no dealings whatsoever with Barletta."

"Are you sure?"

"That she had no dealings with Barletta? Absolutely sure."

One down. Damn.

The only way to find out whether Barletta had drawn up a will was to ask his notary. But perhaps in order to ask a lawyer for information about a client one needed authorization from the courts. So Montalbano rang Tommaseo. A woman whose voice he didn't recognize answered.

"Inspector Montalbano here. I wanted to talk to Prosecutor Tommaseo."

"He's not in."

"Do you know where I can reach him?"

"Listen, just leave him alone."

How dare she?

"And who are you, if I may ask?"

"A colleague of his. Call back day after tomorrow."

"I haven't got all that time to waste!"

"I don't know how I can help you. My colleague was taken to the hospital."

"When?!"

"This morning?"

105

"Why, what was wrong with him?"

"He had a malaise."

The guy probably looked at the photos and had an out-and-out stroke!

"Can I ask you something?"

"Of course."

"Is a notary sworn to secrecy concerning his clients?"

"Naturally."

"So if I need information on one of his clients, I need to ask for authorization?"

"That seems rather elementary to me."

"Thank you. If you see Dr. Tommaseo please give him my best wishes for a speedy recovery."

And above all take those photos away from him, he thought.

Immediately afterwards, it occurred to him that he had nothing to lose by giving the notary a ring just the same. If the guy refused to talk, too bad, he would simply wait for Tommaseo to recover.

But what was the notary's name?

Giovanna had told him. He tried to remember.

Pirrocco? Pissipo? Pitino? Nah, it wouldn't come to him.

The best thing was to call her and ask her for his name.

"Good morning, signora. Montalbano here."

"Good morning. What can I do for you?"

"Am I disturbing you?"

"Never mind about that."

"I need to know the name of the notary whom your father—"

"His name is Piscopo."

"Thank you. That was all I needed."

"Mind you, there's . . ." She hesitated a moment, then continued. "There's no will with the notary."

"And how do you know that, if I may ask?"

"Arturo told me, after calling him yesterday."

So the son had wasted no time finding out how much of the estate was his, before there'd even been a funeral.

"So can we assume he didn't draw up a will?"

"No, I don't think that's the case, either."

"So what *is* the case?"

"Listen, Inspector, couldn't we meet and discuss these things in person? Because I too . . ."

She broke off again.

"You too . . . ?"

"Have a favor to ask of you."

"Could you come to the office at four o'clock this afternoon?"

"All right."

"Ahh, Chief! Ahh, Chief!"

This was the jeremiad that Catarella customarily intoned when " 'izzoner the c'mishner," as he called him, was on the phone.

"What is it?"

" 'Izzoner the c'mishner's onna line! 'E wants

t'know if you—'oo'd be yiz—are in yer affice 'cuz as insohow 'e wants to talk t'yiz."

"And you're going to tell him that you looked for him far and wide in this building and couldn't find him."

" 'oo's 'im, Chief?"

"Him's me, naturally."

"*Matre santa,* I din't unnastan' a ting!"

The inspector hung up.

At ten to one he went home to fetch Livia.

Instead of letting himself in with his key, he rang the doorbell. He liked it when Livia came and opened the door and greeted him with a kiss as soon as he went in.

He was quite surprised to see her in a dressing gown and wearing an apron to boot.

"Why are you still not dressed?"

"Surprise! I've already been into town, I went shopping, and I made lunch!"

Getting clubbed in the head from behind would have been better.

A sort of nostalgic, melancholy canticle passed through his head, a Manzonian sort of thing that went as follows:

Farewell, sea-scented surmullet, fried so light by Enzo's hand they lift you up to heaven! Farewell . . .

"What's wrong? You look so pale."

He quickly seized upon her words.

108

"Yeah, I actually don't feel well," he said, closing the door and putting a hand over his stomach.

"What do you feel?"

"Terribly nauseated. For the last hour or so. I'm afraid I won't be able to enjoy your . . . What a shame!"

Livia was disappointed.

"Come into the kitchen, at least, and see . . ."

"No, no, I really don't feel like it, I'm sorry. I think the smell would only aggravate—"

"But it's a wonderful smell! For the first course I made spaghetti with clam sauce!"

"I don't doubt that the smell must be heavenly, but, believe me . . . Look, let's do this. You go and eat, and I'll wait out on the veranda for you to finish."

"At least keep me company while I—"

"Forgive me, but it would only make me feel worse."

It was better to fast.

Not once in her life had Livia ever cooked pasta properly. Ninety-nine percent of the time it came out all squishy and disgustingly soft. And the other one percent it was still as raw as if it had just been shipped out of the pasta factory.

Or it was either so salty it became bitter, or so insipid that you felt as if you were swallowing worms.

No, it was a thousand times better to go hungry.

* * *

He did, however, have a cup of coffee with her. Then he looked at his watch. It was three.

"I have to go back to the office."

"But do you feel up to it?"

"No, but I have to go. There's an urgent matter that can't wait."

He got in his car and drove off wildly.

It was three-twenty when he screeched to a halt outside of Enzo's trattoria.

He dashed in like a bat out of hell, to the point that Enzo got scared.

"What is it, Inspector?"

"Nothing, I'm in a rush. Just bring me a big platter of antipasti."

"Just antipasti? I was frying up a few mullets for myself and I—"

"Okay, but in the meantime bring me some antipasti."

He stuffed himself and didn't get to the station until ten after four.

8

"Ah, Chief! 'Ere'd a happen a be the signora—"

"I know. Show her into my office."

As she entered, Giovanna flashed a big smile. Jesus, what lips, what teeth! She looked even more elegant than the last time, but beautiful as always.

She was wearing an austere suit with the skirt down to her knees.

Which meant that when she sat down, she displayed her beautiful, very long legs, on which the inspector, against his will, dutifully let his eyes linger. At any rate, she no longer had dark circles under her eyes, having apparently recovered from the initial shock of her father's death.

"I'm sorry if I made you wait, signora, but something unpleasant came up and I got detained."

The rest of the statement should have been: . . . *when Livia, my girlfriend, whimsically decided to cook up a meal and I, to avoid the mortal danger, had to go and eat a late lunch at a restaurant.*

But of course he never said this, and so Giovanna immediately replied:

"No problem!"

And she smiled at him again.

She certainly had quite a mouth!

"You know, I really didn't feel like talking about the will over the phone," she began. "The nanny was around . . ."

"I understand."

"Remember when I told you there'd been a rift between Papa and Arturo over his last will and testament?"

Those were her exact words, "last will and testament."

"Yes, I remember perfectly well."

"Well, the Sunday after that, Papa told me he'd done it."

"Made a will?"

"Yes."

But hadn't she been unsure the last time she mentioned it?

"Was your brother also present?"

"No, not that time. But Papa said he would tell him the following day."

"So what did he do, pick up a sheet of paper, write out his will by hand, sign it, and put it in an envelope with the classic words *My Last Will* written on it?"

"Something like that, actually. I think he left what they call a holographic will."

"So why didn't he solicit the help of his friend the notary?"

"I don't know what to tell you."

"So there must be a will lying around somewhere, either in the beach house or at his place in town."

"I think so. In fact Arturo is biting his nails waiting for the seals to be removed so he can start looking for it."

"Well, I can save him some effort. Tell him we searched the beach house and didn't find it."

Giovanna didn't seem surprised.

"You searched the house?"

"Yes."

"And the one in town?"

"They're still searching it. They're up in the attic now."

"I don't think they'll find it there. Papa would have kept it in a drawer of his desk."

She smiled, a bit mischievously.

"That's where he kept all his secrets."

Montalbano decided to prod her a little.

"Like the pornographic photos, for example?"

She took it rather well. In fact, she seemed amused by the whole thing.

"So you have them now?"

"Not any more. The prosecutor has them."

Her smile became even more mischievous.

The inspector had the impression she'd made a slight movement, and in fact her skirt had come up a little.

"Have you looked at them?"

If you want to provoke me, two can play that game.

"Just enough to know. Have you?"

"I had a sneak peek at them, just once. You can imagine, it's a little unpleasant to see one's own father . . ."

But she didn't seem the least bit disturbed by this.

"To get back to the will," said Montalbano, "if, in the end, we can't find it, what then?"

"Arturo explained to me that in that case the inheritance would be equally divided between the two of us. As if Papa had died intestate."

How many technical terms the lady knew!

"So, in concrete terms, your father's wishes would be disregarded."

"Precisely."

Montalbano quite purposely made a risky move.

"So your brother in the end will have benefited from the disappearance of the will."

"No doubt about it." But then, immediately afterwards: "But please, not so fast, Inspector. There's no need to jump to conclusions."

Good Signora Giovanna, you really know how to throw a stone and then hide the hand that threw it!

"You said on the phone that there was something you wanted to ask me."

"Ah, yes. But first there's something else I need to ask you. When you searched the house in the country, did you find a little box containing a ring with a circle of diamonds on it? It's not terribly valuable or anything, but you know how it is . . . I'm very fond of it."

"I sent my second-in-command to search the house."

"Do you know whether . . ."

"I can ask."

He called Augello's cell phone from the landline and put the speakerphone on.

"How are things coming along?"

"We got started barely half an hour ago. It'll be another couple of hours before we're done."

"Any sign of the will?"

"None."

"Listen, Mimì, when you searched the beach house, did you happen to see a little jewelry box with a ring inside with a circle of diamonds on it?"

"Yes, it was in the upstairs bathroom and it fell on the floor and got stuck behind a piece of furniture. It wasn't easy to find."

"Who's got it now?"

"We left it on the sink."

Montalbano hung up.

"Did you hear?"

"Yes. Can I ask a favor of you?"

"Go ahead."

"Can I go and get it myself?"

"Signora, the seals are still up at the house."

"But isn't there any way to . . . ?"

"We would have to ask the judge for a—"

"But that would take too long! And I need it

right away! Especially if they left it out in plain view."

Montalbano didn't quite grasp the meaning of her last words. He was about to ask her for an explanation when she got up in a huff and went over to the window.

Her tight skirt left her posterior spheres in plain view.

"What's the hurry?" Montalbano asked, getting up and standing beside her.

"I don't want my husband to see that ring," she said in a soft voice, still looking out the window. "It could trigger a tragedy! Our marriage might fall apart."

She had a lover! Someone rather wealthy too! Which explained the designer clothes, the nanny . . .

Then she turned and took one step towards the inspector. She was now so close that he could feel the heat from her body and her breath on his face.

"You really can't do anything for me?"

Montalbano shuddered imperceptibly and stepped back into a safer zone.

"You see, signora . . ."

"I beg you."

She came closer again.

"Do you have the keys to the house?" Montalbano asked her.

"Yes. I have them right here."

"Listen, I could . . . but . . ."

"But?" she asked anxiously.

"I would have to come with you."

"You have no idea how grateful I would be!"

And the long, deep look she gave him made Montalbano start to sweat.

They drove to the house in separate cars so that Giovanna could head back to Montelusa after picking up the ring.

The inspector removed the seals and Giovanna unlocked the door with her key. It was dark inside, since the shutters were all closed.

Montalbano flipped the light switch but nothing came on. Somebody must have turned off the power.

"Do you know where the fuse box is?"

"Behind the house. But we can open the windows."

Without waiting for Montalbano's permission, she opened one, then headed for the staircase. She went up first, and he followed behind.

Upstairs was total darkness. Montalbano stopped, and she went into the bathroom and opened the shutters.

He heard her cry out:

"It's not here!"

Then he went in.

There was nothing on the sink, no little jeweler's box.

But the biggest surprise was the change that came over Giovanna. She was as pale as a corpse, bug-eyed, and muttering a sort of litany:

"Ohmygodohmygodohmygod . . ."

She ran over to the inspector, embraced him, and leaned her head on his chest.

"Help me, oh please help me!"

"Now, now, that's enough of that," said Montalbano, trying to free himself from her perilous embrace.

But she wouldn't let go, and squeezed him even tighter.

The floor under the inspector's feet started to give out.

"If you'd please let me make a phone call . . ."

She took a small step back, leaving him just enough space to move. He searched his pockets but, not finding his cell phone, he said:

"I have to go downstairs to call."

But then she quickly pulled her own cell phone out of the small purse she wore slung over her shoulder and handed it to him.

As Montalbano was bringing the phone to his ear after dialing the number, she brought her face close to his to hear what was being said.

"Mimì, listen . . ."

"Oh, Salvo, I tried you at your office but Catarella said—"

"Mimì, the little box . . ."

"That's exactly why I called you. I wanted to

tell you that I remembered putting the box in the top drawer of the armoire, under the shirts. I didn't want to leave it anywhere too visible."

She gave a start and dashed out of the bathroom.

Montalbano lost a little time wiping his brow and closing the window. Then he went into the large guest room where he remembered seeing an armoire. But Giovanna wasn't there.

So he went into the main bedroom, the one Barletta used to sleep in.

The armoire was open, the drawer with the shirts was pulled halfway out, and Giovanna was standing there with the little box in her hands.

"I found it!" she said happily.

The inspector held out his hand. She quite clearly pretended not to understand.

"I want to see the ring."

"But I told you! It's a—"

"I want to see it."

Giovanna opened the box and was about to take out the ring, but Montalbano prevented her. He reached out and grabbed the box. She looked at him in shock.

It was a common jeweler's box. He opened it. Inside the dark-green felt lid were the words, in gold: *Marco Falzone Jewelers—Montelusa.*

The ring was tasteful in design and, contrary to what Giovanna had said, must have been very expensive.

He gave her back the box with the ring inside. She put it in her purse.

"Shall we go?" Montalbano asked.

She looked at him. But was she really looking at him, or were her eyes simply planted on him while her thoughts were elsewhere?

"Okay," she said after a pause, then headed for the stairs.

She didn't give even a passing glance to the bed where her father had spent his last night in the company of a woman. Then she stopped suddenly, turned around, and ran into the other bedroom.

Taken by surprise, Montalbano lost a few seconds before following her.

Since she hadn't opened the shutter, the inspector didn't so much see her as guess that she was lying across the double bed, her face buried in a pillow.

She was sobbing.

He went over to the window and let a little light in. He turned around. Giovanna, still in the same position, raised her right arm and called him over to her, waving her hand.

She wanted consolation.

Never, not even for all the gold in the world, no matter how much he would have liked to, would he have lain down on the same bed as her.

"I'll wait for you downstairs," he said.

He went down, opened the front door, and

closed the shutters. He heard her start to come down the stairs. Waiting for her by the door, he signaled to her to go out, but when she was right in front of him, she suddenly turned and pressed her lips against Montalbano's cheek. She held them there longer than necessary, pressing harder and harder.

"Thanks," she said.

This was undoubtedly one of the cases in which he'd been most kissed by women.

They went out, and she locked the door. The inspector put the seals back up.

She opened the passenger's-side door to her car and held her hand out to him. Montalbano shook it, but then Giovanna wouldn't let go. She kept looking him straight in the eyes.

"Would you come out to dinner with me one of these evenings?"

"Yes," said Montalbano.

Livia, after all, was leaving.

As it was too early to go home, he dropped in at the station. Immediately Fazio came into his office.

He was about to speak but then stopped short and gawked at him.

"What is it?" asked the inspector.

"Nothing, nothing," Fazio said evasively.

"What do you have to tell me?"

"I think I've found the guy's name."

"And what would that be?"

"Giuseppe Pace, who had a nice shoe store but turned to Barletta for a loan and had the blood sucked out of him. His wife is in a treatment center in Montelusa. She's not really crazy, but isn't quite all there anymore."

"So it all fits."

"So it would seem."

"Do you have the address?"

"Go and get him for me. How long will it take you?"

"If he's home, I'll be back in half an hour."

While the inspector was waiting, Mimì Augello came in and put a rather large cardboard box down on his desk.

"I'm all covered with dust. I'm gonna go take a shower."

"Did you guys finish?"

"Yes."

"Find any other threatening letters?"

"No."

"The will?"

"Nothing. But are we so sure there actually is a will?"

"Beats me. Probably not, even though he told his children he'd made one."

Then, glancing at the box, Montalbano said:

"What's in there?"

"All of Barletta's amorous correspondence. Or at least all the letters and notes he received."

"Was it in the attic?"

"No. Since you'd planted the seed in my mind, I went and started rummaging around in his desk. You know what it's like, don't you? It looks like a castle. It seemed like something he inherited from his great-grandfather. And then it occurred to me that these kinds of desks have secret drawers. Well, I got down to work and found two. One of them contained letters from one woman, six in all; the other had the letters from everyone else."

"How were you able to tell that the ones in the first drawer were all from the same woman? Are they signed?"

"No, they're not signed. But you can see that they're all written by the same hand."

"Did you read them?"

"No, there wasn't time."

"Then read them. Those and all the others."

"That's a lot of work. Listen, Salvo, it's getting late. I'll do it in the morning."

"There's another thing I need to ask you. How was he able to take those pictures without anyone knowing?"

Mimì explained how.

"Hello, Chief?"

"What is it, Fazio?"

"I went to Pace's house and rang the bell, but there was no answer. So I asked a neighbor lady for some information and she told me that Pace always goes and spends the night in Montelusa, at his daughter's place, and comes back in the morning around nine. What should I do? Go to Montelusa? I have the address."

"No, there's no need. Just bring him in to me tomorrow morning, around nine-thirty."

"Sorry, Chief, but what if the guy runs away in the meantime?"

"Why would he run away? If he hasn't done so by now . . ."

"Maybe he found out we're searching Barletta's homes and, knowing he'd written him a compromising letter . . ."

"I'll take responsibility for it. Go and see him tomorrow."

"Whatever you say, Chief."

By instinct, by sense of smell, the inspector felt that the motive for Barletta's double killing was not revenge on the part of some poor bankrupted bastard, but something far more complex.

Since he'd put everything off until the next day, he headed home to Marinella.

When he walked in shortly after seven, Livia, as he'd imagined, wasn't there.

Maybe she'd gone off to pester the hobo.

He had to tell the poor guy that Livia would soon be leaving. Otherwise the man was likely to pick up in despair and find another cave to live in.

124

Anyone who decided to live that way didn't likely do so as a natural choice. Clearly circumstances had brought him to such a pass, and normally people like that wanted nothing to do with the rest of humanity.

So then why go and bother him, pretending to be driven by feelings of charity, when in fact it was only pure and simple, egotistical curiosity?

He sat down on the veranda with a glass of whisky in one hand and his cigarettes and lighter in the other.

It was a lovely evening, beautiful enough to soften the hearts of mariners and mountaineers alike.

9

He couldn't help thinking about the circumstances of Barletta's murder. All at once he remembered something he'd completely ignored concerning the poison that had been put in the victim's coffee. But to get the information he needed he would have to phone Pasquano—there was no getting around it, even if it meant being buried under a hail of insults.

He got up, went inside, and dialed the doctor's home phone number.

A woman answered. It was his wife.

"Montalbano here, signora. I would like to speak with your husband."

"You know he's eating at the moment?"

The wife's question was in reality a polite warning that could be translated as follows: "Are you aware of the risk you're taking?"

Indeed, by direct personal experience, he knew that disturbing Pasquano as he was having a meal was exactly like trying to take a gazelle out of the mouth of a hungry lion.

"I'm sorry to insist, signora, but . . ."

"All right, then," the woman said, resigned.

The phone must have been near the dining room, because the inspector distinctly heard her say:

"It's Montalbano on the phone."

At once a sort of powerful animal-like roar or, better yet, an elephant-like trumpeting, blasted in his ear. Montalbano was ready for such a reaction; otherwise he might have simply hung up in fright. Then the trumpeting turned into an enraged human voice:

"Tell him to go—"

"You tell him," said his wife.

That Pasquano had grabbed the receiver was clear to the inspector from the sound of grinding teeth he heard at the other end.

"So a man can't relax at home and eat a quiet dinner without you coming and busting his balls! You know what? You're not a human being but a cojones-crushing robot!"

"Listen, Doctor—"

"Do you know what's my highest aspiration in life? To perform your autopsy!"

"Forgive me, Doctor, but—"

"No, I won't forgive you! On the contrary, I damn you for all eternity! What the goddamn motherfucking hell do you want?"

"That paralyzing poison you told me about, the one used to kill Barletta, where do you find it?"

"Where do I find it? What kind of stupid fucking question is that? Is your mushy brain incapable of formulating a question with even a bare minimum of common sense?"

"What I meant was: Can one buy it at a pharmacy?"

127

"No, you have to go to the supermarket. Sometimes you can find it at local fairs, at the peanut stands!"

"Doctor, please!"

"No, you can't get it at a pharmacy. It's used in very small doses in hospitals."

"Can you tell me what it's called?"

"Are you capable of writing it down?"

"I can try."

He dictated the name to him, breaking it down syllable by syllable. And he concluded:

"And now you can go and take it up the—"

The inspector hung up.

The fact that the poison was used in hospitals wasn't, after all, such bad news.

He'd just gone back outside and sat down on the veranda when he heard the front door open and close.

He got up and went inside to greet Livia.

The events that followed would probably be best appreciated if they were recounted as in a movie screenplay:

> Full shot. Livia and Salvo come together in the middle of the room. They are both smiling.
>
> Tight close-up of Livia's face. Her smile suddenly vanishes.
>
> Tight close-up of Salvo, who stops

smiling, surprised and wondering why Livia is no longer smiling.

Full shot. Both standing there, not moving, staring at each other.

Detail of Livia's right arm being raised.

Close-up of Salvo's face receiving a violent slap.

Livia's voice off-camera: "Disgusting pig!"

Full shot. Livia running out of the scene. Salvo brings a hand to the slapped cheek and stays like that.

Tight close-up of Salvo, hand still on cheek, bewildered, confused, incredulous.

But what had gotten into her? Had she lost her mind? This was the first time she'd ever dared to whack him like that! Why did she do it? He was as innocent as Christ!

Burning with rage, he shook himself and went after her. She'd locked herself in the bathroom.

"Open up, Livia!"

No answer. He shook the doorknob violently.

"Open the door!"

Still nothing. Furious, he drove his shoulder hard into the door, which didn't move one millimeter.

He stepped back, got a running start, and put his shoulder again into the door. It hurt like hell, and on the other side of the door the whole bathroom shook; but, other than that, the result was nil.

"If you don't stop I'm going to call the police!" Livia shouted.

"Don't be ridiculous. *I'm* the police!"

"Then I'll call the carabinieri!"

He stopped in the middle of a second run towards the door.

This was a serious threat. He mustn't do anything stupid. If the carabinieri intervened, the whole thing was sure to end in farce.

He gave the door a final kick, but without conviction, and abandoned his assault.

He decided then and there to take the car and go eat somewhere alone.

Outside the bedroom there was a mirror. As he passed it, he instinctively looked at himself.

And he realized why Livia had slapped him.

Planted on his right cheek, in lipstick, were two female lips.

They belonged to Giovanna, who'd kissed him as they were leaving Barletta's house.

That was why Fazio had given him such a strange look! But why hadn't he felt the need to let him know?

He went back and pressed against the bathroom door.

"Livia, believe me, I can explain everything."

He had to dig in and be patient. Livia was capable of staying behind that locked door for hours.

When, forty-five minutes later, Livia saw fit to open the door, she took one look at him and locked herself back in.

"Come on, Livia! Don't start again!"

"Get that disgusting lipstick off your face!"

"But if you won't let me into the bathroom, how can I—"

"Go wash it off in the kitchen!"

He turned on the faucet, washed his face, and dried it with a dishcloth that stank from reuse.

Livia, meanwhile, had gone and sat down on the veranda. She was staring out at the sea.

"Can I sit down?"

She kept on staring at the sea. Observing the rules of the silence game, Montalbano sat down in front of her.

"You're blocking my view."

Which meant he could sit down beside her.

"Want to hear my explanation?"

"I'm not interested."

"I'm sorry, but if you're not interested, why did you slap me?"

"Because you're a pig."

"Do you want to hear the pig's side of the story?"

"So you admit you're a pig."

"Just so you'll listen to me."

She said nothing in reply, and he told her the whole story of Barletta's murder. As he was speaking, Livia became more and more interested, to the point that halfway through she stopped staring at the sea and started looking at him. She interrupted him only once, when he told her about the photographs that Barletta took of the girls.

"Were they all consenting?"

"A few."

"And how did he do it with those who were against it?"

"He photographed them secretly. Mimì, who'd searched the man's two homes, explained to me that he had placed two remote-controlled cameras on top of the armoires in the bedrooms of the place in town and his beach house. More recently he'd started using his cell phone as well."

"Go on."

In the end she said:

"I'm sorry."

And she threw herself into his arms.

Montalbano had neglected to tell her one utterly negligible detail: that when Giovanna had invited him to dinner, he'd immediately accepted.

Their reconciliation followed all the rules governing the reconciliation between a man and a woman who truly love each other. Thus when Montalbano got out of bed, it was ten-thirty, and he was ravenous with hunger. But before they could wash and get dressed, another hour would go by, and they wouldn't find a single restaurant still open.

He went into the kitchen. Opening the fridge, he found large passuluna olives, cheese, caciocavallo, and prosciutto, which Livia had apparently bought when she'd gone shopping.

There was enough for a meal. But he'd better get it ready quick, before Livia got it into her head to make some pasta!

When he'd finished setting the table on the veranda, he went and called her.

"I went to see Mario this afternoon," she said as they were eating.

He didn't know any Marios.

"And who's that?"

"What do you mean, 'Who's that?' He's our friend in the cave."

He knew it! She'd gone and bothered the guy again!

"Listen, Livia, I think it might be better if you didn't . . . I think that man would rather be left alone."

"You're wrong."

"Why?"

"Because he talks to me. He clearly likes to talk. He's glad I come to see him. You know what he said as soon as I came in? 'I was expecting a visit from you.' Don't you see?"

"Has your curiosity been satisfied?"

133

"No. He never says anything about his past life. And I'm not sure I was able to satisfy his."

"What was he curious about?"

"You."

Montalbano balked.

"Me? What did he want to know?"

"He didn't ask me directly, but I could tell he wanted to know about what kind of person you were, how you behaved in certain circumstances, if you were an understanding person, that kind of thing."

Montalbano felt puzzled by the hobo's interest in him. Maybe the guy had committed some crime and wanted to take advantage of the situation to talk to him about it man to man?

"He also told me something that I didn't quite understand at the time, because I didn't know anything yet about the murder of this Barletta guy."

"What did he say?"

"He said he'd met the guy five years ago, when he used to live near Barletta's place in the country. Then he moved to another area and never ran into him again."

They finished eating. Livia cleared the table; Montalbano helped, and then they went and sat down in front of the television, which Montalbano turned on.

The purse-lipped face of Pippo Ragonese, the

chief newsman for TeleVigàta, materialized.

. . . and so, from the information that has leaked out, it would appear that Ragioniere Barletta was, paradoxically, killed twice, by two different killers. But in this tragedy there's a comical element that we can't help but point out: that of the two killers the brilliant Inspector Montalbano hasn't been able to find even one! This may be due to the—

The inspector never did find out what this was due to because Livia suddenly got up and changed the channel.

"Why do you just sit there listening to that jackass?"

"It's amusing to me."

"Amusing! So you're also a masochist!"

"What do you mean by 'also'? What am I besides a masochist?"

"The list would be too long and I feel like watching a film."

"I'm sleepy; I'm going to go to bed," Livia said when the film was over.

Montalbano lingered a little while longer, watching the television. As soon as he heard her come out of the bathroom, he went in. When he was ready for bed and entered the bedroom, he saw Livia, naked, standing on a chair and feeling around on top of the armoire with her right hand.

"What are you doing?"

So, not only a masochist but also a voyeur or whatever it was called? He leapt forward, grabbed her around the waist with a rugby tackle, and dropped her down on the bed.

Later, Livia said:

"Tomorrow's my last day here, so we can laze around in bed all day."

"You can, but I can't."

"Why not?" she asked, disappointed.

"I'm sorry," said Montalbano.

And he really was sorry.

"But I have an appointment tomorrow morning."

"With that woman—what's her name—Giovanna?" asked Livia, sitting up, ready for a fight.

"Calm down. And don't start again. I'm seeing a man who wrote Barletta a threatening letter."

Livia looked doubtful.

"I don't believe you."

What a pain in the ass, this jealousy!

"I swear it's true!"

"Give me a break!"

What could he do to persuade her? He had an idea.

"Listen, here's a solution. I'm going to wake you up tomorrow morning when I get up and you can come to the office with me. That way you can see with your own eyes whether I'm telling the truth or not. Now give me a kiss."

· · ·

At eight o'clock the following morning he shook Livia gently, to wake her up.

"Mmm?"

"Time to get up."

"Mmm?"

"Remember we agreed you'd come to the station with me this morning."

"Bah!" she said, turning onto her other side and going properly back to sleep.

As I was saying, thought the inspector.

Giuseppe Pace was a run-down, shabbily dressed man of about sixty.

At first glance the inspector was convinced the man was quite incapable of killing anybody.

"Signor Fazio explained why you wanted to see me. I swear to you, Inspector, I wrote that letter in a moment of . . ."

His eyes began to tear. He tried to finish his sentence but was unable.

His chest suddenly started heaving with sobs.

What am I doing torturing this poor wretch? Montalbano wondered.

He looked over at Fazio, who returned his glance. They'd spoken with their eyes, and Fazio had told him he was in agreement about the poor man. In fact Fazio said, in a neutral voice:

"I found Signor Pace in church. He had a mass said for the soul of Barletta."

"No, sir, you're wrong! I had it said for my own soul," Pace intervened. "For the wicked thoughts I had when I was wishing death on that unhappy man!"

"You considered him unhappy?"

"Not at first, no. But after I wrote that letter to him, I started thinking about what the man really was. And he was a poor, unhappy wretch! One who would never find peace! His life was hell on earth! The more he had, the more he wanted! Nothing was ever enough for him: money, women . . . Isn't a man like that unhappy?"

At the sound of these words, Montalbano felt something churning inside.

Pace had gone beyond forgiveness. He'd come to discover, and understand, and pity, the profound, endless unhappiness there was in the soul of the man who had been tormenting him to death.

Maybe those whom church people call saints are like that, he thought.

He couldn't think of any words to say.

Fazio was the one to speak up, after clearing his throat.

"I also wanted to tell you that Signor Pace has an alibi. He spent the night between Saturday and Sunday, when Barletta was killed, at the hospital, because his wife had tried to kill herself. I didn't verify, but I can even check from here whether . . ."

"I sincerely apologize for having bothered you, sir," said Montalbano, springing to his feet. "I won't keep you any longer. Fazio, please give the gentleman a lift wherever he has to go."

Even all the way to heaven, he wanted to add.

"Will you need me afterwards?" Fazio asked.

"No. Have a good day."

What now? If he went home too early, Livia was sure to kick up a row.

"If it was a matter of only ten minutes, couldn't you have postponed it?"

"You see, Livia . . ."

"No, you did it on purpose to spend the least amount of time possible with me!"

On the other hand, he couldn't just stay in his office twiddling his thumbs. Catarella wasn't even there to help pass the time; it was his day off.

All right, then, he would deal with Livia's resentment. He might dispel her bad mood by suggesting they take the car and go out to Fiacca for lunch, since there wasn't a cloud in the sky.

He left. As he was about to take the curve before turning onto the small road that led to his house, he saw the vagabond coming down from his cave. Pulling the car over to the side of the road, he braked and got out. The man was right there.

"Good morning, Inspector."

He was wearing Montalbano's suit, shoes, and one of Adelina's shirts as if it was the most natural thing in the world. Apparently he was used to dressing well.

"Good morning. I wanted to apologize to you."

"For what?"

"Well, Livia may not realize . . ."

"No, not at all! She's an exquisite person! I love her visits!"

"She'll be leaving tomorrow, and so . . ."

"I'm sorry to hear that. Will you be leaving too?"

"No. If you need anything, you know where to find me."

"Thank you. I may even take advantage of your kindness. Have a good day."

"You likewise."

The inspector got back in his car and started it up.

Why, when he spoke to that man, did he always feel a little awkward?

10

He was sticking his key in the lock but Livia beat him to it and opened the door. She was all dressed up.

"I heard your car pull up. So that was all you had to do at the station? You weren't there very long!"

Better change the subject immediately.

"Where are you off to?"

"To catch the bus to Vigàta. I called Beba—it was so long since we'd spoken—and since it's so nice and sunny this morning, we decided to get together."

"When will you be back?"

"I'm not coming back, because you're going to join us . . ."

What was this?

". . . for lunch at their place."

Already decided and etched in stone. Without deigning to ask his opinion.

The prospect of eating with Mimì Augello and his wife Beba didn't exactly thrill him. The truth of the matter was that he simply didn't like having lunch at other people's homes, with rare exceptions. As a cook, Beba was passably decent, but the fact was that if you're invited to lunch,

141

you necessarily have to make conversation; you can't just sit there in silence. Whereas he, when he ate, didn't feel like talking.

Mimì, moreover, to justify some of his nocturnal escapades, often blithely told his wife he had to go out for work assigned him by his boss. If Beba were now to ask him about one of her husband's nighttime missions, he might very well get confused and say the wrong thing, and the whole gathering would take a nasty turn.

"Listen, I'm so sorry, but I really won't be able to make it to lunch at Beba's," he said decisively.

"Why not?"

"Because I have to do something later and I have utterly no idea when I'll finish. But, if you want, I can give you a ride there."

Livia got into the car.

"You'll be free this evening, at least?"

What did that question mean? Want to bet she'd organized some other pain-in-the-ass activity for them? Better cover himself.

"Listen, I won't know until after I've done what I need to do. At any rate I'll call you on your cell phone and let you know."

"Because Beba really wanted us all to go and see a film. She's really keen on it."

He'd been right to cover himself. Beba had terrible taste in films.

They found Beba outside her front door.

"How's Salvo?" asked Montalbano.

Salvo was Beba and Mimì's son, whom they'd named after the inspector.

"I left him with my mother, who's staying with us for a few days."

So Augello's mother-in-law was there, too. She was a good woman whose only defect was that she talked without interruption from morning till night. Mimì'd told him she even talked in her sleep.

Well, that was a close call! He would have had to eat against a background of constant chatter!

"Salvo, unfortunately, won't be able to join us for lunch," Livia said to Beba.

"I was afraid of that!" said Beba.

"Why?" Montalbano asked out of curiosity.

"Well, since you summoned Mimì for a twelve-thirty meeting I figured that you, too . . . ," Beba replied.

Montalbano immediately realized that Mimì had had the same idea as him! He'd told his wife a whopper to avoid coming to lunch!

"Why didn't you tell me that Mimì also wasn't—" Livia started to ask him.

"It slipped my mind. But maybe it's better this way. Now you and Beba can talk about girl stuff far from male ears!"

He kissed Livia and Beba good-bye and dashed off.

• • •

Once he was out of their range, he called Mimì on his cell.

"Where are you?" he asked him.

"At headquarters."

"What are you doing there?"

"Jack shit. I'm just hanging out here because—"

"I know why you're there. Because I summoned you for a twelve-thirty meeting. But you're early!"

They laughed.

"Where are you going to eat?" asked the inspector.

"Dunno."

"Listen, wait for me to get there."

Mimì was waiting for him in the parking lot.

"Get in. I'll take you to Fiacca," the inspector invited him. "We'll have some nice lobster—you have no idea how much I've been wanting some. It feels like a hundred years since I last ate lobster."

"Okay," said Augello. "But let's do things right. You get in my car."

"Why?"

"Salvo, if we take yours and you drive, at your cruising speed we won't get there till three."

During the drive there, Montalbano asked:

"Did you have time to look at the letters?"

"Yeah, I looked at them, but not the six that

were in a separate drawer. Those are long and seemed like they needed to be gone over very carefully, without haste. But I read all the ones that were in the other drawer, and, believe me, there were a lot."

"And?"

"Well, in fact there were probably only about ten proper letters in all."

"It looked to me like there was more than that."

"There was, but the others were all little messages of one or two sentences. And ninety percent of them weren't signed."

"What did they say?"

"Most of them involved the moment when Barletta got tired of the girl and started skipping the meetings. 'Why didn't you show up yesterday?' Or, 'If you treat me the way you treated me last time, I don't know if I'll come or not.' I even recognized some notes from Stefania, which were real ballbusters."

"But why did they write to him instead of calling him?"

"I wondered the same thing until I read a note that said, 'Since you won't answer your phone . . .' Get it? When he was getting ready to dump one of them, the first thing he would do was stop taking their calls."

"And what about the letters?"

"Four of them, all in the same handwriting, are quite interesting but not for the investigation."

"Then in what way are they interesting?"

"For knowing Barletta's sexual preferences. In each letter the woman gives a kind of review of everything they did the last time they saw each other. And she makes some suggestions as to what to do the next time. I have to admit, they both had a lot of imagination."

"And the other letters?"

"There are only two that seem in some way important."

"Are they signed?"

"No. In the first one the girl senses that Barletta is going to leave her, in the second she's sure of it. And in reading the second one you realize she's actually in love with him. The letter ends by saying that if he dumps her, he'll pay dearly."

"Mimì, how can you say that letter 'seems in some way important'? It seems extremely important to me! It's a death threat!"

"Salvo, it's a death threat made by a woman."

"So what does that mean?"

"Look, Salvo, I've received at least three such threats and I'm still here driving you to Fiacca."

"Well, I want to see them anyway."

"I'll bring them to you tomorrow."

"And read the others too, I mean it."

"As I was reading those letters and notes," Mimì said after a pause, "I remembered the photos I saw and tried to play a kind of game, but it didn't really work."

"And what was that?"

"To match certain letters and notes with some of the girls photographed. But I was unable. One thing's certain, though, which is that photographing every girl he'd taken to bed seems to me like a pretty insane thing to do."

"Mimì, when you were a little kid, did you collect stamps?"

"No, but I don't see the connection."

"Well, you should. This is just another collection mania. A lot of sex maniacs have it. They say that D'Annunzio used to keep specimens of pubic hair of all the women who had passed through his hands, in a cabinet made specially for that purpose."

Then he fired a barb at his friend:

"Strange that you, who love women so much, don't—"

"I like them in the flesh," Augello said, cutting him off.

Some ten minutes later, another question occurred to the inspector:

"But did Barletta have a safe in his house?"

"Yes. One at home in town and another in the beach house. Not proper safes, really, but walled strongboxes of the kind you usually hide behind a painting."

"Did you open them?"

"Yes."

"Where did he keep the keys?"

"Both in the same place: in the drawer of the nightstand in the bedroom."

"What was in them?"

"In the one in the country, just ten thousand euros; in the one in the apartment, two hundred thousand euros, a Rolex, and some jewelry."

"Did you draw up an inventory?"

"Yes, in duplicate. Sent one copy to Tommaseo."

"So apparently nothing was stolen. The murder motive could not have been theft."

"So it seems."

At the restaurant, Mimì tried to put some Parmesan cheese on his pasta with clam sauce, but Montalbano grabbed his wrist and threatened to cut his hand off if he dared commit such a sacrilege.

The lobster they served the inspector was a true delight.

Mimì, who wasn't big on seafood, had ordered a piece of rabbit cacciatore.

In short, they had a good time of it.

On the way back, Montalbano asked Mimì:

"What are you doing later?"

"Well, tonight I'm going to the movies with our women. What about you?"

"Pay close attention, so you know what to say later."

The inspector took his cell phone out of his pocket and rang Livia.

"Hi. Unfortunately, as I'd expected, I can't come to the movies with you. I did manage, however, to free up Mimì, so you'll be in good company. So what's the plan?"

"I'll be home by ten," said Livia, hanging up.

"So if they ask what our engagement actually involved—you know how curious they are— what should I tell them?" asked Mimì.

"Tell them we were on a long stakeout that came to nothing, and that's why I have to stay on. Now take me to the office."

"And what'll you do this evening?"

"There's a film with De Niro and Pacino showing in Montelusa."

"And what if the women decide they want to see it, too?"

"Nah, come on! Beba wouldn't dream of suggesting a film like that!"

When he unlocked the front door of his house it was half past nine. And Livia, naturally, arrived punctually at ten.

"But, do you do it on purpose?" was all she said when she saw him.

"Do what?"

"Wait for me here at home. How long have you been here?"

"Since nine-thirty."

"But our rendezvous was for ten! Just like last

149

time! Half an hour's difference matters! You just want to make me feel guilty!"

"Are you kidding me? I do not do it on purpose! Think for a second. This is my house. Am I not free to come home whenever I want? Why do we always have to fight?"

"I'm sorry, I'm a little on edge and talking nonsense."

"Why are you on edge?"

"Before coming home I went to see Mario and I realized that he was unwell. He had a touch of fever. I'm worried about having to fly home tomorrow morning and leaving him there all alone. Will you promise me—"

"All right, I get it. I promise I'll go see how he's doing tomorrow, either in the morning or in the afternoon."

"Did you eat?"

"A sandwich. You know how it is, on a stake-out . . ."

Livia knit her brow.

"How is it then that Mimì said he had rabbit cacciatore?"

The asshole!

"Well, I made him go and eat. I could carry on the stakeout by myself for a short while."

Livia swallowed the lie. Montalbano changed subject.

"So what film did you guys see?"

"Some teenage love story, totally trite. It was

already obvious from the title. But Beba wanted to see it, and so . . ."

"Listen, where are we going to eat?"

"Are you really up to going out again? It's our last night together. Are you hungry?"

"Well, having had only a sandwich . . ."

"Let's see what there is in the kitchen. If there's enough, I'll make something myself. What do you say?"

"I say that's a great idea," said the inspector. "Go and see."

He was unconcerned, having checked before she came home. And indeed, moments later, Livia emerged from the kitchen looking rather disappointed.

"I'm afraid we really do have to go out," she said.

"Damn!" exclaimed noted hypocrite Salvo Montalbano.

He took her to Enzo's.

"We're in something of a hurry," said Livia.

"I'll make you wait as little as possible," Enzo promised.

Two hours later, they were back home.

"Shall we have a drop?" Livia suggested.

As she was opening the French door to the veranda, Montalbano went and grabbed a bottle of chilled white wine for Livia and the whisky bottle for himself. They sat down beside each other on the bench. Livia drank half a glass and leaned her head on Montalbano's shoulder. He then reached out with one arm and wrapped it around her waist.

And they stayed that way, drinking in silence and enjoying the night.

The following morning he drove her to Montelusa to get the seven o'clock bus to Palermo's Punta Raisi airport. Montalbano hugged her so tight, and held her so long, that Livia became concerned.

"What's wrong?"

"I'm sorry you're leaving."

"But are you okay?"

"I'm great, don't worry."

But it wasn't true.

He could tell he would miss Livia a lot.

On the drive back, he was overcome by a great wave of melancholy.

This always happened to him when Livia went away, but this time it was stronger than ever before.

A sign of aging?

This time, along with the melancholy, there was also a twinge of personal malaise that he couldn't explain.

Since the weather that morning was so beautiful it looked fake, he turned onto a dirt road, drove about a hundred yards, stopped the car, got out, and started walking through groves of almond and Saracen olive trees, the latter somewhat rarer.

Then all at once he realized why he felt the way he did. This time, the sadness he felt over the departure of his beloved was magnified by an awareness of how alone he was.

His was a loneliness crowded by all his colleagues in the police department, but it was still loneliness.

He spent almost every evening of his life alone; he ate alone; he went for walks alone. He didn't have a single friend to talk with about things that mattered to him, to ask for advice, to confide in.

He used to like this situation. Solitude gave him a feeling of freedom. Lately, however, it had started to weigh on him.

Deep down, what difference is there, he thought, *between my life and that of the hobo in the cave?*

Don't be silly, the other Montalbano promptly cut in. *For starters, one difference is that your life is useful to others, while the hobo's is useless. On top of this, the hobo was probably forced into solitude by circumstances, whereas your solitude is the result of a free choice. Like yesterday, when you did your own thing even though Livia was around. And when you get so tired or scared of your solitude that you can't take it anymore, all you have to do is call Livia and she'll be there, dependably, at your side.*

He felt somewhat reassured.

And it was certainly because of this line of reasoning that when he got to Vigàta, he continued on to Marinella to pay a call on the man in the cave.

"How are you? Livia told me yesterday you had a little fever."

The man was sitting on the broken chair. He stood up when the inspector entered. They shook hands.

"I just checked it again, and it's going down. No need to worry. It's just a common flu. But keep your distance, please. I wouldn't want you to catch it."

"Would you like me to take you to see a doctor?"

The vagabond smiled.

"A doctor wouldn't tell me anything I don't already know."

A little pretentious, their friend.

"Do you need any medicine?"

"I have some aspirin, thank you."

Montalbano didn't know what else to say. The other broke the silence.

"The lady left?"

"Yes."

"Take good care of her."

Montalbano looked at him, a bit perplexed.

"She's a rare jewel."

Livia was a good, kind person, and he loved her from the bottom of his heart, but a rare jewel? Then the man seemed to read his mind.

"You know, it's not uncommon that after one has been with another person for a long time, their ability to see that person's qualities fades a little."

This was true.

But it was also true that this man was himself an extraordinary person.

"Well," said Montalbano, "I should go. Let me repeat that if there's anything you need . . ."

"I'll certainly be down to see you, don't worry about that. But that would be premature now."

Why premature? What did he mean by that?

He must have meant something. The guy never talked just for the sake of talking. But there was no point in pressing him.

Montalbano shook his hand and went off to the station.

11

"Ahh, Chief! Ahh, Chief, Chief!"

Whenever Catarella said this, it meant 'izzoner the c'mishner had called. And the fact was that the commissioner had already called and Montalbano'd had Catarella tell him he wasn't there. He couldn't keep pretending not to be in.

"What did he want?"

" 'E called juss now! An' 'e tol' me ta tell yiz 'at as soon as ya do like wha' the Madonna does . . ."

The inspector balked.

"Is that what he said?"

"Nah, nat azackly, Chief, bu' sints I fuhgot wha' 'izzoner the c'mishner said azackly, I tought 'at mebbe if I mintioned the Madonna ya might figger out wha' 'izzoner the c'mishner said. Know what I mean?"

"No."

"Sorry, Chief, the quession might seem kinda priestly, but wha' does the Madonna do?"

"She performs miracles."

"No, no, Chief. 'A'ss not it, if you'll forgive me sayin' so. 'Izzoner the c'mishner din't say nothin' 'bout miracles. But 'e said the same ting 'at the Madonna did at Lourdies in France."

Montalbano had a flash, perhaps by the Madonna's good graces.

"You mean she appeared?"

" 'Ass azackly it, Chief, ya got it right! 'Izzoner the c'mishner tol' me a tell yiz atta minnit ya 'peered inna affice, you's a sposta call 'im straightawayslike."

"Okay, I'll call him later. Is Fazio here?"

"Yeah, 'e's onna premisses."

"Send him to me."

"Yeah, Chief?"

"Listen, Fazio, do you remember when, right after Barletta was killed, I told you I wanted to know everything about him and his son Arturo?"

"Of course I remember."

"Well, at this point I know more about Barletta than I would ever want to know, but it seems we've forgotten about Arturo."

"That's true. But I made up for it."

"What does that mean?"

"I spent yesterday working on him."

"Excellent! Find anything out?"

"Yessir."

Fazio stopped and made an appropriate face.

"Can I look at the piece of paper I have in my pocket?"

"If your intention is to read me some of those personal particulars that you're so goddamned obsessed with, forget about it."

"They're not personal particulars."

"Then all right."

Fazio took out a sheet of checked notebook paper and looked at it.

"Remember when Arturo told us he was married with no children?"

"Yes."

"Arturo's wife, Michela Lollo . . . ," he began, then, all at once, extremely fast: "daughter of Giuseppe Lollo and Concetta Virzì, born in Montelusa on the twenty-fourth of April, 1980, and residing in Vigàta in a—"

"Are you fucking kidding me?" the inspector interrupted him. "Do you realize what you're reading?"

"Sorry," Fazio said hastily. "I got distracted."

He put the piece of paper back in his pocket.

But he was satisfied. At least he'd managed to smuggle in one piece of records-office information.

"Apparently this Michela is a fine-looking woman. She married Arturo when she was twenty-two."

"If I remember correctly, Barletta didn't get along with his daughter-in-law."

"From what I found out, that wasn't quite the case."

"Oh, no? Then what was the case?"

"It was Arturo who didn't want his wife to frequent his father."

"He was afraid Barletta couldn't keep his hands off?"

"As far as that goes, Signor Barletta's hands had already been on Michela."

Montalbano was stunned.

"Really?"

"Well, I can't really swear to it on a stack of Bibles, but, at any rate, people say Arturo fell in love with Michela when the girl was still his father's mistress. Got that?"

"I'll say."

"Barletta meanwhile got tired of Michela, and so when his son said he wanted to marry her, he didn't make any fuss."

"So then why didn't Arturo want—"

"Because after they got married, Barletta's old passion for Michela was rekindled and Arturo noticed."

"But did the rekindling burn anything?"

"I don't understand."

"Did Barletta manage to get her back?"

"Nobody could say for certain. At any rate, from that moment on, Arturo arranged things so that his wife would have no more contact with his father."

"Wait a second: Was all this happening when Barletta's wife was still alive?"

"Naturally."

"Naturally? Does something like that seem natural to you?"

"No, Chief, it doesn't. It's just a manner of speaking."

"Did they tell you whether the wife was aware of her husband's continuous infidelities?"

"I didn't ask."

"Is there anything else?"

"Here's the best part. This Michela immediately became friends with her sister-in-law, Giovanna. And so she started asking Arturo for money so she too could dress up in designer fashions and jewels and drive fancy cars—"

"Stop right there. I don't think Giovanna's husband makes so much money, either . . . What do people say about that?"

"That Giovanna has long had a rich lover."

"Do they know his name?"

"I didn't ask. Anyway, Arturo, who had only his miserable salary, immediately started accumulating debts. And not only with the banks."

"Did he turn to loan sharks like his father?"

"Yes he did. And he'd lately been pretty scared after he started getting some serious threats when he was no longer able to make his payments on time."

"Did Barletta know about his son's situation?"

"Of course."

"So why didn't Arturo turn to him?"

"First of all, he wasn't so sure his father would pay his debts. Barletta forked out money only

160

if there was a profit to be made in cash or fresh flesh. And, secondly, he may have been afraid."

"Of what?"

"That Barletta would only give him the money on one condition."

"What?"

"That Michela be allowed to see him again, so to speak."

"With her husband's permission?"

"With her husband's permission."

"In front of everyone?"

"In front of everyone. After all, what the hell did Barletta care? He was a man capable of anything, with no sense of morality, restraint, dignity, honor—nothing. A real stinking bastard."

Nice little portrait, no doubt about it. But a perfect likeness. A snapshot.

"Anything else?"

"Isn't that enough?"

"For now, yes."

"And yet I have one more thing to tell you."

"And you saved it for last?"

"That's right. Like the big bang at the end of the fireworks show."

"Let's hear it."

"Do you remember when Arturo told us he worked as an accountant?"

"For a Montelusa construction company, I think."

"Exactly, Sicilian Spring, it was called."

"And so?"

"A couple of weeks ago this company sent out a letter to all its employees announcing that it is ceasing all its activities at the end of the month and that therefore everyone—stonemasons, clerks, and everyone else—has to take a hike."

"Why are they closing?"

"The contractor ended up in jail when they discovered he was a front man for the Mafia."

"I see. So Arturo found himself in hot water up to his neck."

"That's right."

When Fazio had finished, Montalbano took stock of all he had just heard.

"The obvious conclusion is that only his father's inheritance could get Arturo out of the trouble he was in. In fact the guy went crazy trying to find out whether his father had made out a will. But this will is nowhere to be found, not at the notary's or at either of the father's two residences."

"Bear in mind that we have no evidence against him."

"I just meant it rhetorically speaking. But I would pay a little more attention to him anyway."

"Tell me what you want me to do."

"Right now I don't know. Let's you and I meet here tomorrow morning at nine, and we'll go and have another look at the beach house."

• • •

"Ah, Chief! 'Ere'd be a call onna line from a lady 'at calls 'erself Giovanni Pistateri."

"But is it a man or a woman?"

" 'Ass a difficult quession, Chief, insomuch as iss a maskerline name, bu' the verse is fimminine. Mebbe iss the seckertary o' the fersaid Giovanni Pistateri or mebbe the wife o' the fersaid Pistateri or the sister o'—"

"Why not the mother?"

Catarella thought about this for a moment.

"The fimminine verse sounds perty young, Chief, f'rit to be the verse o' the mutter o' the fersaid Pist—"

The inspector had had enough fun.

"Okay, you can put the call through."

Click.

"Signor Pistateri?"

"Pusateri. Do you prefer me male?" said the voice of Giovanna Barletta.

Only then did Montalbano remember that Pusateri was her husband's name.

"Let me ask you again: Do you prefer me male?"

"What are you talking about? I like you exactly the way you are!"

Giovanna gave a mischievous giggle.

"I was worried for a moment there," she said. "How are you?"

"I'm fine. And you?"

"I'm fine too."

There was a pause. Perhaps she wanted Montalbano to take the initiative.

"I was waiting for you to call," he said.

"Really? How?"

"What do you mean, 'how'?"

"Anxiously? Impatiently? Indifferently?"

"I would rule out 'indifferently.' "

"Good sign. And, as you can see, I have called."

"Does your invitation still stand? Or have you changed your mind?"

"You don't know me very well, Inspector, but I do hope you'll have a chance to get to know me a little better. When I say something, I mean it. I'm unlikely to change my mind. So, yes, my invitation still stands."

"I'm glad."

"But you decide on the time and place, please. I'm not familiar with the restaurants."

He couldn't think just then and there where to take her. It was better to play for time.

"Listen, Giovanna, I have to check and see whether a particular establishment is open tonight. Could you come by here this evening at eight?"

"Okay."

There was no getting around it. The time had come to phone Commissioner Bonetti-Alderighi.

"Catarella? Get me 'izzoner the c'mishner on the line, would you?"

"Straightaways, Chief."

It used to be that while waiting for a telephone connection he would review the multiplication tables in his head. The problem was that he'd gone over them so many times that he now knew them all by heart, and it was no longer any fun. So, what could he do to pass the time? How about the *Iliad*? He began:

> Sing, goddess, the anger of Peleus' son
> Achilleus . . .

"Inspector Montalbano, are you on the line?" asked a voice he didn't recognize.

"Yes."

"Please wait just a moment."

> . . . and its devastation, which put pains
> thousandfold upon the Achaians,
> hurled in their multitudes to the house of
> Hades strong souls
> of heroes, but gave their bodies to be the
> delicate feasting of dogs, of all birds . . .

He heard some kind of click.

> . . . and the will of Zeus was accomplished . . .

"What are you saying, Montalbano? The will of who?"

"I'm sorry, Mr. Commissioner, I was asking someone about the last will of . . . a . . . some person—"

The commissioner cut him off.

"Come to my office at once."

Click.

He headed off to Montelusa cursing the saints, knowing that he would come out of the meeting all agitated, as happened whenever he came out of a meeting with the commissioner.

The only consolation was that he would not run into Dr. Lattes, chief of the commissioner's cabinet and a notoriously boring buttonholer, in the waiting room. He'd heard that the doctor was on holiday.

The assistant showed him in at once.

As soon as he entered he noticed that Bonetti-Alderighi was smiling. The commissioner had two ways of delivering bad news: either by smiling or by frowning darkly.

Either way, the guy was still a blockhead.

"Please sit down, my good man."

If he was asking him to sit down and calling him "my good man," it meant the news must be dire.

"How's the investigation into the Barletta murder going?"

"One small step at a time, sir, because . . ."

The guy wasn't listening.

"Have you got any idea yet who did it?"

"In a way . . ."

"Prosecutor Tommaseo certainly has."

Montalbano bristled. Was the guy going to listen to him or not? If he didn't want to know how the investigation was going, why had he busted his balls by summoning him to Montelusa?

He decided that it was best to ignore his anger and start amusing himself instead.

"Really?" he said.

"Did he have a chance to explain it to you?"

"Oh, has he recovered? I heard he'd had a slight malaise."

"He's fine now. So you haven't had a chance to meet with him?"

"Actually I've had no—"

"Do you think the prosecutor's opinion is somehow unimportant?"

"Good heavens, sir! On the contrary I think it is supremely valid and of absolutely utmost importance . . ."

Easy on the superlatives, Montalbà!

"Well, if you don't know his theory, then I'll lay it out for you."

"I'm all ears," said the inspector, leaning his upper body forward and sliding his buttocks to the edge of the chair.

"In his opinion, Barletta was killed by one of his young mistresses who was jealous of the mistress

167

who later killed him in turn because she, too, was jealous of the one who did away with him."

Montalbano buried his head in his hands. What was this shit coming out of the prosecutor's fevered brain?

"What's wrong?"

"I'm trying to understand, Mr. Commissioner."

"I'll try to explain a little better. Let's call Miss A the young woman who, the morning after sleeping with Barletta, served him the poison because she was jealous; and we'll call the other mistress, the one she's jealous of, Miss B. Clear so far?"

Montalbano pretended to have suddenly regressed to the grade-school level.

"Maybe you could write it out for me on the blackboard . . . ," he suggested in the faintest of voices.

"Are you raving? What blackboard? How can you not understand? I'll repeat it for the last time: Miss A kills Barletta with poison because she's jealous of Miss B. Miss B in turn shoots Barletta because she's jealous . . . of whom? Come on, now, Montalbano, what's the answer?"

So he really was in school. Montalbano kept on playing the role of the dim-witted schoolboy.

"Miss C?" he said questioningly.

"Miss C? What are you talking about? It's because she's jealous of Miss A! Is that clear now?"

"Frankly, I don't . . ."

The smile returned to 'izzoner the c'mishner's face. A sign of maximum danger.

"Now, as you will have managed to notice, there are a great many girls involved in this affair, most of whom cannot be easily identified."

Where was he going with this? It seemed like a good moment to express agreement.

"Right," said the inspector.

"It so happened that as Prosecutor Tommaseo was explaining his theory, Inspector Mazzacolla of the vice squad was also present. Do you know him?"

"I haven't yet had the pleasure. Has he been here long?"

"He started working the day before yesterday."

"And what did Mazzacolla say?"

"He didn't say anything. But seeing how interested he was, I had an idea I wanted to try out on you."

So the commissioner was also getting ideas?

"Please try it out on me."

"To slice the Barletta case into two parts."

"Meaning?"

"Assigning Inspector Mazzacolla the task of identifying the girls, always under the direction of Prosecutor Tommaseo, of course."

"And me?"

"You will continue to investigate the alternate

leads, while keeping in mind that the management of the case—"

Montalbano couldn't resist continuing to play dumb.

"There's a whole management staff?"

"Come on, Montalbano! Of course there's not! Try to understand for once! By the 'management' of the case, I meant simply the general direction . . ."

"I'm sorry, I get it."

"At any rate, bear in mind, I repeat, that the preferred lead to follow will be that of the girls."

"May I make an observation?"

"Go ahead."

"I'm convinced that of all the girls who had relations with Barletta, only two or three, at the most, were prostitutes. The rest are salesgirls, students, and so on . . ."

"So?"

"So I wonder what's the point of bringing in Inspector Mazzancolla—"

"Mazzacolla."

"—of the vice squad, who just got here, on top of everything else."

The smile vanished from Bonetti-Alderighi's face.

"That's a decision that's of no concern to you, is that clear? It was as a courtesy to you that I let you know beforehand of a move I will make the moment you leave this office."

12

At this point, he had no choice but to play the part of someone who has been profoundly, unjustly wronged. It was a role he usually pulled off rather well.

"Ah!" he said.

And he stood up, making a bitter face.

Then he stared long and hard at Bonetti-Alderighi, shook his head, and repeated:

"Ah!"

The second "Ah" was quite plaintive.

The commissioner cast him a questioning glance.

Now the inspector had to choose the right words.

He opened and shut his mouth twice without making a sound, as though his throat was dry from the injustice suffered, then cleared his throat noisily. At last he spoke.

"Allow me to say that I cannot help but see, on your part, a lack of confidence in my actions as a scrupulous functionary of the state, if you want to take a slice away from me!"

And he shook his right arm in the air a few times, folding it back and forth in a kind of slicing motion.

"Come now, Montalbano, things are not —"

171

"A slice is still a slice, you know."

"I realize that, but—"

"And on top of that, it's the main slice!"

"Listen, Montalbano—"

"I'm upset, Mr. Commissioner, if I may say so! Upset and offended! Good-bye."

He turned his back and left the room.

He wasn't the least bit agitated, on the contrary.

He'd put on a show of being offended, but in reality he was pleased.

As he'd foreseen, Tommaseo was going to throw himself on the trail of the girls like a starving dog after a bone and give them no rest. And that way he himself would be free to work in peace without having to report or explain anything to the prosecutor.

Entering headquarters, he asked Catarella if Augello was in.

" 'E ain't been onna premisses all mornin', Chief."

"Did he call?"

"No, sir."

"Then get him on the line and put the call through to me."

The telephone rang immediately.

"Hello, Mimì? What's going on?"

"Sorry, Salvo, but I forgot to inform you I wouldn't be coming in this morning."

"Are you unwell?"

172

"I feel great. I stayed home to read those letters you mentioned, the ones that were in the separate drawer."

"And it's taken you all morning to read them?"

"They merit a lot of attention, believe me."

"So when will you be coming around?"

"Five o'clock this afternoon okay with you? At three I have to take Beba and Salvo to—"

"Okay, okay."

Before going out to eat, he remembered he had to call Adelina to let her know that Livia had gone home to Boccadasse and that the coast was therefore clear.

His housekeeper heaved a long sigh of satisfaction, then asked mischievously:

"Didda young a leddy mekka you goo' tings ta eat?"

Montalbano decided not to enter into the subject.

"We always ate out."

"Then I come a by inna aftanoon to mekka the bed an' clean a house 'at the young a leddy alway leave a so filty iss like a pigga house, ann' enn I cooka you sometin a for a tonigh."

If Livia had heard Adelina say she left the house as filthy as a pigsty, she would have demanded that he immediately fire his housekeeper. On top of everything else it was hardly true that Livia neglected to clean the house; this was simply a fixation of Adelina's—or rather, a continual defamation, one worthy of criminal prosecution.

"Don't make anything for tonight, because I'm invited out."

"Ah, Chief!" Catarella hailed him as he was passing by on his way to the parking lot.

"What is it?"

"I wannit a give yiz a messitch from yer goilfrenn Miss Livia 'oo jess rung yiz onna phone."

"Why didn't you put the call through?"

"Miss goilfrenn Livia tol' me assolutely not to distoib yiz 'cause alls I neetit a tell yiz wuzza messitch 'at she got to Genoa okay ann' 'at she wannit a remine yiz not to forgit to visit the sick man."

He noticed that Catarella seemed a little awkward.

"Have you got anything else to tell me?"

"Nah, Chief, 'ass alls was inna messitch. But . . ."

"Come on, man, speak!"

"Ascuse me fer bein' so bole, Chief, but I gotta ax yiz a quession: Are ya also a dacter?"

"What do you mean 'also'?"

"I mean also a middical dacter?"

"Are you kidding?"

" 'Enn why's Miss Livia want yiz to go an' visit a sick man?"

174

"Cat, Livia means for me to pay him a visit and keep him company."

Catarella looked disappointed.

"I's thinkin' utterwise. 'Cuz if you was also a middical dacter I's gonna tell yiz about dis stiff neck I got 'at rilly hoits allot an' . . . ."

Montalbano ran away.

At Enzo's he kept to mostly light stuff in view of the meal he would be having that evening with Giovanna. He thought he would take her to that trattoria on the beach between Montereale and Sicudiana, whose specialty was every kind of antipasto the heart desired. However, even though there was no need, he took his regular walk along the jetty out to the lighthouse.

Sitting down on the flat rock, it occurred to him that the dinner with Giovanna was coming at exactly the right moment, just after everything Fazio had told him about Arturo.

And for her part, Giovanna herself, with more than a little skill and grace, had managed to insinuate a few less than edifying things about her brother Arturo.

Therefore, if there really was a will, then the only person who had something to gain by making it disappear was Arturo.

According to what Giovanna said, the will granted her the better part of the inheritance and left the smaller part to Arturo. Also according to Giovanna, Barletta had made this decision because she had two children while Arturo had none.

But it's possible the real reason was something else entirely.

Barletta may have been taking revenge on his son for not allowing him to carry on his love affair with his former mistress, who had become Arturo's wife.

But the reasons that had led Barletta to make that kind of will were not terribly important. The important thing was that the disappearance of the will was to Arturo's advantage, since in that case, by law, the inheritance had to be divided equally.

This did not mean, however, that Arturo murdered his father.

Augello came in at five-thirty, instead of five o'clock, as he'd promised.

"Do you know what time it is, Mimì? It's five-thirty."

"Yeah, I know, I'm sorry, but—"

"Half an hour is half an hour!"

He realized he was repeating Livia's reproach when she chided him for coming home too early.

Mimì sat down, took six letters bound by a rubber band out of his pocket, and handed them to the inspector.

"Should I read them myself or will you tell me what's in them?"

"For the moment I can tell you about them, but I think you'd do well to have a look at them later yourself."

Montalbano put them in his jacket pocket.

"So tell me."

"A preliminary statement. These six letters have no envelopes that might tell us who sent them, and they are not signed. From our perspective, they're totally anonymous. The only thing they have in common is the handwriting. They're all written by the same person and must have been fairly important to Barletta, for him to keep them hidden in a secret drawer."

"You've already told me this."

"Yes, but it's good to remind oneself. Even though they're not dated, it's clear they cover a rather long span of time."

"How long?"

"In my opinion, about ten years."

"So long? How can you tell?"

"Well, over time a person's handwriting tends to change in certain ways. And that's what happens in these letters. Then there are some references in the letters themselves that make you realize this."

"Are they love letters?"

"In a way, yes. I don't know whether there really was any love between the two, but there was certainly a strong physical attraction."

"Strange."

"Why?"

"Because normally Barletta's affairs lasted three or four months at the most. After which he would get tired of the girl and find another."

"Well, he never got tired of this one, that's for sure. She may be the exception that proves the rule."

"I'll forgive you the cliché. Go on."

"There's one letter above all that seems extremely interesting to me. It's very clear. The woman doesn't speak in metaphors. And you realize that, after not frequenting each other for a very long time, chance brought them back together, alone . . ."

". . . and without suspicion," said Montalbano.

But Augello didn't catch his scholarly quotation of Dante.

". . . for a few hours. And they couldn't resist."

"It happens."

"Yes, it happens, but it's not that often that one such encounter happens to have a serious consequence."

"Namely?"

"She got pregnant."

"A pretty pickle! So how did it turn out?"

"The letter that follows explains everything."

"What does it say?"

"It says that despite the advice that Barletta—"

"Wait a second. How do these letters begin?

With his name? Or do they say, 'My darling,' or 'My love,' or something similar?"

"No, there's nothing like that. She always gets straight to the point. You'll see for yourself."

"Sorry, go on."

"At any rate, Barletta must have advised her to get an abortion, and she wrote back that she wanted to have the baby. And it's clear that she wins out in the end."

"So we're dealing with a young single mother."

"Not necessarily."

"Why do you say that?"

"Because she often refers to a man she's living with."

"Does she ever mention him by name?"

"No."

"Does she ever say explicitly that he's her husband?"

"No."

"So it might just be someone she shares a flat with."

"I suppose. But when she tells Barletta she wants to keep the baby, she tries to persuade him by saying, in so many words, that neither he— that is, the person who lives with her—nor any of the others will ever suspect that Barletta is the real father."

"In short, she kept the baby and led everyone else to believe that the father was her husband or the man she lived with."

"Exactly."

"And afterwards, how does her relationship with Barletta evolve?"

"They have their ups and downs. What comes out of the letters is that they both do their best to break off the relationship, but they can't live without it. Whenever they get the opportunity, they end up together in bed."

"And there's nothing that might give us even a little clue as to this woman's identity?"

"Salvo, why do you think I spent all that time on those letters? No, there's nothing at all."

"Do you think she did it on purpose?"

"Did what on purpose?"

"Took all these precautions to prevent anyone from recognizing her, in case the letter ended up in the wrong hands?"

"I'm absolutely convinced she did it on purpose!"

"Tell you what, Mimì. I'm going to take those letters home with me tonight and read them. And we can discuss them again tomorrow."

At five minutes to eight the phone rang.

"Ahh, Chief! 'Ere's 'at lady 'at sez 'er name is Giovanni Pustateri onna line!"

What? Had something come up?

"What is it, signora?"

"Inspector? I'm so sorry, but I'm going to be

late. The nanny had been to see her sister in Montereale and called just now to say she's on her way, and I don't have anyone else to leave the kids with."

"No problem at all, signora. I can wait."

"I won't be more than half an hour late."

"Nowadays, being half an hour late isn't late at all."

Wait a second! He was being inconsistent! He'd reproached Mimì for being late, just as Livia had reproached him for being early! Half an hour was half an hour!

Indeed. What could he do during that half hour of waiting?

Read a letter, for one thing.

He took them out of his pocket, removed the rubber band holding them together, took the one on top, and started reading. From the very first lines he realized he was looking at the important one. Mimì hadn't bothered to put them in a hypothetical chronological order.

A little over two months have passed since that afternoon when a combination of lucky (or unlucky) circumstances brought us back together in an embrace that immediately shut out the world around us. It was as though the years of separation—which we'd both wanted, but hadn't sought—had never happened. Our two bodies immediately recognized each other and fused in a sort of vibrant inevitability . . .

A bit rhetorical, but the girl wrote pretty well. The telephone rang. He set down the letter and picked up the receiver.

"Ahh, Chief! 'Ere'd a happen a be summon calls hisself Mazzancolla 'at wants a talk t'yiz poissonally in poisson!"

"Over the phone?"

"Yessir."

"Put the call through."

"Montalbano? This is Fabio Mazzacolla. I trust the commissioner has informed you that he assigned me a section of the Barletta case two days ago."

Therefore 'izzoner the c'mishner had already done the deed when he spoke to Montalbano, and the whole bit about giving Mazzacolla the assignment the moment the inspector left the office was a big fat lie. But there was probably no point in picking a fight with Mazzacolla, who had nothing to do with it.

"You mean his breaking up the Barletta investigation into two sections? Yeah, he told me everything."

"Well, since I think the two sections of the investigation should proceed in parallel fashion, but not independently of each other, it seems it would be helpful if there was an ongoing exchange of information between the two of us. Don't you think so?"

No, I don't, he felt like answering.

Instead Montalbano the hypocrite said, in a joyous tone of voice:

"I think that's an excellent idea!"

"I knew you would agree. If you like, I can begin to brief you."

Why not? After all, he had to kill some time before Giovanna arrived.

"Brief away."

"So. In the meantime I must tell you that earlier this afternoon something happened that made us all rather uneasy. This morning one of the people working with me, when he saw the photos of the girls—"

"But how many people have you and Tommaseo shown those photos to?"

"Well, five or six. Certainly the bare minimum."

"You should try to be very careful."

"In what sense?"

"In the sense that you could cause trouble."

"Meaning?"

"Mazzacolla, most of those girls are not professional prostitutes."

"I'm well aware of that."

"Say one of the girls who frequented Barletta because she was momentarily desperate for money but then stopped got engaged to be married and is now living a respectable life. You, by busting your way into her private life, could—"

"Unfortunately it's already happened."

"*What* has already happened?"

"It's what I was saying. One of my coworkers this morning thought he recognized one of the girls, but at the time he couldn't remember where he'd seen her and in what circumstances. As soon as we got back to work after lunch, my coworker suddenly remembered having seen her in Mandorliti's office and—"

"Who's that?"

"Mandorliti? You don't know him? He's an assistant commissioner, the new chief of the antiprostitution office."

"Got it, go on."

"So, my coworker and I, drawing the wrong conclusion, were convinced the girl was a prostitute. And so I authorized my coworker to show Mandorliti a few photos so he could tell us who she was."

"And who was she?"

"She was Mandorliti's niece!"

"Holy shit!"

"You have no idea of the shitstorm! The guy raced to the commissioner's office wanting my head. It took some doing, in short, to calm him down. But I wouldn't want to be in that girl's shoes."

"What did I say?"

"Listen, I have to tell you about another discovery we've made. I need to brief you on this too."

"Go ahead."

"Over the phone?"

"Well, isn't that what you've been doing up till now? Briefing me over the phone?"

"Yes, but this is sort of, how shall I say, a different matter. Perhaps it's better if I come to you."

"When are you thinking of coming?"

"Now."

"Now?!"

13

At that moment Catarella appeared, signaling from the doorway that he needed to talk to the inspector. With a wave of the hand, Montalbano invited him to enter. Catarella approached with the stealthy step of a cat burglar, circled round the desk, came up practically behind him, bent down, brought his lips to the inspector's ear and said, in a low conspiratorial voice:

"The Signora Giovanni Pustateri jess now arrived poissonally in poisson."

"Bring her in here," the inspector replied, just as conspiratorially, meanwhile covering the receiver with his hand.

"Montalbano? Are you there?" said Mazzacolla at the other end, no longer hearing any sound.

"Sorry, Mazzacolla, I dropped a sheet of paper on the floor . . . You were saying?"

"That I'll be dropping by your office."

Giovanna came in, well dressed and looking gorgeous. Montalbano gestured to her to make herself comfortable. She sat down in such a way that the slit on the side of her skirt exposed her legs, which in any case merited attention.

"I'll be there in about twenty minutes," Mazzacolla continued.

Out of the question! All he needed was this

Mazzacolla in his hair! He had to find a good excuse. Giovanna meanwhile was passing the time looking around.

"Are you still there, Montalbano?"

Man, was the guy ever in a hurry! At last an idea came to him.

"No, listen, I'm very sorry, but you really can't come right now! It's just not possible, I mean it! I'm in the middle of an important interrogation . . ."

Giovanna cast him an admiring glance.

". . . which I broke off momentarily, but only for the time needed to answer your call."

"I could come later."

Good God, was this Mazzacolla ever desperate to brief someone!

"Look, you'd be putting yourself out for nothing. I already know I'm gonna have my hands full all night with this interrogation."

Giovanna, who by now had caught the drift, put a hand over her mouth to stifle a laugh.

"Okay, then, I'll come by tomorrow morning, if I can."

"All right."

He hung up, smiled at Giovanna, who smiled back, got up, and started to pick up the letter he'd been reading, but then it fell to the floor in front of the desk. Giovanna bent down, picked it up, and handed it to him. Montalbano put it with the others, stretched the rubber band around them, and put the packet in his pocket.

"Do you really intend to interrogate me all night?" Giovanna asked with an innocent, angelic look on her face.

"If need be . . . ," said Montalbano, standing up.

She did the same.

"Oh my God! And will you give me the third degree?" she asked, pretending to be afraid.

"If necessary . . ."

Giovanna laughed.

"Did you find out whether that place is open?"

"You know I totally forgot to call? Wait just one minute while I . . ." he said, hand poised over the telephone.

"Don't do it," she said.

"Why not?"

"Let's just go there anyway."

"And what if it's closed?"

"We'll look for a different place."

"And what if we don't like it?"

"Then we'll look for another."

"So we'll just go hunting in the dark?"

"Don't you think that would be fun, to go hunting in the dark with me?"

Signora Giovanna didn't miss a single opportunity to try to provoke him. Better not follow her down this perilous path. He dodged the question.

"Shall we go in my car or yours?"

"Do we pass by your place on the way to the restaurant?"

"We pass right in front of it."

"Then let's leave here in two cars, and you can park yours at home and get into mine."

As he was passing by Catarella's closet, the telephone receptionist called him aside.

"Can I ax yiz a quession, Chief?"

"You go on, I'll be right with you," the inspector said to Giovanna. "What do you want?"

"Can ya 'splain a me why a lady 'ass a lady like Signura Giovanni's got a man's name?"

"Because her parents wanted a boy, but since they got a girl, they consoled themselves by giving her a boy's name."

"Tanks, Chief! Y'er a reggler encyclapythia! Ya know th'answer t'evverting!"

Montalbano parked his car outside his house, got out, came back down the dirt road that led to the main road where Giovanna was waiting for him, and got in her car.

"You found a beautiful place to live," she said, heading off.

"I got lucky."

"Do you live there . . . alone?"

"Well . . . most of the time."

"What does that mean?"

"Sometimes my girlfriend comes and stays with me."

"Oh. She's not from around here?"

"No. She's from Genoa. She just left, in fact."

He could have refrained from giving her that last bit of information. She hadn't asked anything of that nature, but he wanted to see what she would do with it.

His curiosity was immediately satisfied.

"Listen, if we don't come back too late from the restaurant, will you show me your house?"

"Sure, why not?"

She was a good driver, no doubt about that. Self-assured, precise, and perhaps a bit too speedy for the inspector's tastes.

"Do you smoke?" she asked him out of the blue.

"Yes."

"What?"

Montalbano took out his pack and showed it to her.

"Would you light one for me?"

The inspector lit one, took a drag, and passed it to her. Then he fired one up for himself as well.

"Normally I don't smoke," she said. "I only do it when I feel a little nervous."

"So you feel a little nervous now?"

"I just said I did."

"And why's that?"

"Because I'm with you."

Montalbano pretended not to have understood anything and deflected the ball she'd just passed to him to a corner.

"It's a pretty common phenomenon. Even the most honest people, when they find themselves in front of a police detective . . ."

But she put the ball immediately back in play.

"You didn't understand what I said."

"What didn't I understand?"

"I didn't mean you as a policeman."

When the lady sank her teeth into you, she didn't let up for even a second.

Why was she acting this way? What was her purpose?

Clearly she wasn't doing it because she felt overwhelmed by his charm, even though she was doing everything in her power to make him think this was the reason.

"Now you need to guide me."

Montalbano guided her.

And, naturally, he had her make a wrong turn, and they ended up outside a peasant house with ten or so enraged dogs surrounding their car, barking and baring their teeth.

" 'Oo's there?" said a voice.

"Let's get out of here before they start shooting," said Montalbano.

On second try, they managed to take the right road.

In the distance they saw that the restaurant's neon sign was lit.

After the first five antipasti, Giovanna asked:

"Why so quiet?"

Montalbano chuckled.

"I'm sorry, it's just a habit of mine. I have to confess I don't like to talk while I eat."

"Why not?"

"Because I think I'm better able to savor what I'm eating if I don't talk. That way I'm not distracted."

This time it was she who laughed.

"You find that funny?"

"No, but I just thought of something, and I was wondering whether . . ."

"Whether what?"

"I can't say it. I'm a lady."

"Forgot that fact for a moment."

"Oh, okay. I was wondering whether you also become quiet when you . . . when you make love."

At this point it was clear to even a half-wit that her intention was for the night to come to a specific conclusion. So the question was: Should he give her rope or not?

He decided he should.

"You know what? I really don't know. We could do a test."

She looked at him. She was about to say something but changed her mind and said something else instead:

"These antipasti are truly delicious."

End of first round.

Giovanna was a hearty eater. Montalbano liked women who could enjoy a good meal without worrying about their figure.

She wasn't up to ordering a second course, however.

"I couldn't get even a grape past my lips."

Montalbano didn't order anything else, either.

An assortment of some twenty-odd antipasti and a big platter of spaghetti with clam sauce had sufficed. And they still had a nearly full bottle of white wine, just opened, in front of them.

"Would you like a coffee?" he asked her.

"No. Let's finish the bottle and leave."

"Okay," said the inspector, filling her glass.

"Where are you in the investigation? Provided of course that protocols of official secrecy don't prevent you from telling me . . ."

Giovanna had decided to move to a full-frontal attack.

"Frankly, there hasn't been much progress."

"Are you still stuck at square one?"

"No, of course not. We have managed to take a few steps forward, mostly by process of elimination."

"Could you tell me, again provided that—"

"I really shouldn't. But since you're the victim's daughter . . ."

"What do you mean by process of elimination?"

"First I must ask you a question: Can I feel free to speak of your father without you getting offended?"

"I knew my father quite well, you know."

"Then you must know that he lent money at extremely high rates of interest."

"I was aware of the fact that he was often a loan shark. There's no need to pick and choose your words with me."

"We've managed to rule out that the murder was committed by one of the people he ruined."

"But if you rule out the motive of self-interest—"

"I didn't say that."

"Then I don't understand."

"I'll try and explain."

Here he needed to proceed carefully. One word too many or too few could compromise everything.

"Perhaps we need to look at the self-interest motive within a more limited circle."

She understood at once.

"You mean . . . within the family circle?"

Come on, Montalbano, get that idea out of her head at once. It's still too early talk about that.

"Not only. Your father was very generous

with the girls he went with. It's possible one of them . . ."

Giovanna wasn't biting, however.

"Then how do you explain the fact that there were two killers?"

Indeed, from this perspective, you couldn't explain that fact. *Let's shunt the discussion in another direction without answering the question,* the inspector said to himself.

"Of course, if we could just find the will . . . ," he said practically under his breath, as though talking to himself.

"What's the will got to do with it?"

"A lot. But are you really sure he made one?"

"He told me he did. And I'm certain he did. But explain to me why the will is so important."

"You put me in an awkward position."

"Please."

"If we could find it, it would be better for you and your brother, in that you would be immediately cut out of the investigation."

"Whereas now we're in it?"

"Well, Prosecutor Tommaseo, you see, has no choice but to . . ."

He was expecting a furious reaction. In essence, he was telling her straight to her face that both she and her brother were suspected of patricide. The stuff of Greek tragedy!

Whereas she remained extremely calm.

"Have you conducted a thorough search?"

"Yes. We even discovered two secret drawers in the desk. Did you know about them?"

"No."

First point against Giovanna. That "no" was as fake as the Modigliani heads that were found in Livorno.

Also false was the tone of the question that followed.

"What was in them?"

She knew perfectly well what was in them. Just as she knew that her father kept the photographic documentation of his amatory exploits in the desk as well.

"Letters and messages from the girls he—"

"I get the picture. So now you're going to interrogate all those poor girls who were unlucky enough to have written to him?"

"They won't be so easy to identify."

"They're not signed?"

"Some of them are. But a first name like Silvia or Francesca doesn't get us very far."

"So you haven't been able to trace them back to their senders?"

"No."

"You can't identify them from the photos either?"

"Oh, two or three have been identified, but I don't . . ."

She smiled.

"I guess things are dragging on a little. Would you like my own little personal contribution to the investigation?"

"Yes, please."

"I can't be the one who confiscated the document. When my brother Arturo called me from the beach house at seven-thirty that Sunday morning to tell me that Papa . . ."

The sound inside Montalbano's head was not the ringing of a bell, but the crash of a bell clapper striking his skull.

"Didn't he call at eight?"

"No, it was seven-thirty. I'm quite certain of that. I believe I already told you that the children—"

"Yes, yes, now I remember. They were having breakfast before going to school. But wasn't it Sunday?"

"Of course it was. But their school had organized an excursion for that morning."

"So, you were saying?"

"That when Arturo rang, I was the one who answered. He called me at home, in Montelusa. I'd woken the kids up at seven. So I couldn't very well have entered my father's house before Arturo to confiscate the will. And aside from that, I hadn't set foot in my father's flat in town for a very long time. And I can prove it."

In other words, dear Salvo, what Signora Giovanna is telling you is that nobody but her brother Arturo could have absconded with the will. And that's not all she's saying. She's also leading you down a specific logical path: that is, that in order to steal the will, one had to kill Barletta first.

What's two plus two?

She was indirectly throwing the murder onto her brother's shoulders.

Not content with this, Giovanna threw fuel on the fire.

"On top of everything else, as I said last time, the disappearance works only to my disadvantage . . ."

. . . Whereas my brother Arturo would only benefit, Montalbano finished her sentence in his mind.

There was no wine left.

"Shall we go?" she asked.

For the whole ride back she didn't say a word. Every so often a hint of a melody escaped her fine half-open lips. The wine seemed to have put Signora Giovanna in a good mood.

Suddenly she asked:

"Do I have to make the next turn?"

"Yes."

She pulled up in front of the inspector's house and they got out. He opened the front door, turned on the light in the vestibule, and stood aside to let her in.

"I'm going to show you the most beautiful thing about the house," said the inspector.

He went and opened the French door.

"This is fabulous!"

"Have a seat."

She sat down on the bench.

"Something to drink?"

"No, thanks, I've already had enough. Anyway, I have to drive."

She sat there a few moments in silence, gazing at the sea.

"When I stayed at Papa's house I also used to spend a good hour gazing at the sea before going to bed."

She sighed.

"Think I could have another cigarette?" she asked.

"Are you feeling nervous?"

"No. I also smoke when I'm happy."

He handed her the pack and lighter.

She lit a cigarette, took a puff, passed it to Montalbano, then lit a second one for herself.

"Why don't you come and sit down beside me?"

They sat there close together, smoking.

Montalbano was now expecting her to make a move—her head on his shoulder, a caress of his hand—but it never came.

It was as if Giovanna had suddenly changed her mind.

Maybe she no longer felt like concluding the evening in Montalbano's bed.

Or else she was one of those women who step hard on the accelerator in the early going but then realize they've exceeded the speed limit and start to slow down.

"I really should be going," she said, standing up after stubbing out her cigarette in the ashtray.

Montalbano got up to let her by, then went to show her out.

She did the exact same thing she'd done at her father's house.

She stopped in front of him and kissed him. But on the lips this time. For a long time.

"Thanks for everything," she said.

Montalbano opened the car door for her, shut it behind her after she got in, then waited for her to drive off. Before she vanished at the end of the dirt road, Giovanna stuck her arm out the window and waved bye-bye.

The inspector went inside, ran into the bathroom, and washed his face.

14

Sitting on the veranda, he started thinking about Giovanna's behavior. Undoubtedly the evening had ended better than he'd feared. From the very first moments of their encounter, she'd had a mischievous, provocative, openly inviting attitude. And this had worried him, in as much as he had no desire to follow her down that path. He'd decided to play along because he wanted to understand what was behind her great display of availability. But to play along only up to a point.

Luckily this attitude on her part had changed the moment she set foot in his house, but not because of any change of mood. In fact the whole way back she'd done nothing but hum to herself in the car. Maybe she'd simply decided she no longer needed to keep up the charade she'd been enacting for him up to that point.

Which meant that during the dinner she must have told him what she wanted to tell him or else found out what she wanted to know.

Part one: What had she wanted to tell him?

She'd wanted to tell him that the only person in a position to make off with the will was her brother Arturo, and that therefore he alone could have killed Barletta.

And she'd even unwittingly provided him with proof of this.

Whereas Arturo had always claimed he'd arrived at his father's beach house at eight in the morning, Giovanna maintained he called her at seven-thirty.

"Seven-thirty is seven-thirty and not eight! There's a half an hour difference!"

That was more or less what Livia had said to him. And it was more or less what he'd said to Mimì.

Conclusion: Arturo was inside the house well before eight o'clock.

And she'd also provided an alibi for herself.

Part two: What had she wanted to know?

This was the real question.

Try as the inspector might to remember their entire conversation from the restaurant, he couldn't find a single point where Giovanna had shown greater interest than the others and asked more questions than usual.

So was the only purpose of the evening to put Arturo in hot water?

The telephone rang as he was closing the French door before going to bed.

It was Livia.

"Did you make it home all right?"

"Yes. Didn't Catarella tell you?"

"Yes, he did. Oh, after dropping you off, I went and paid a visit to our friend."

"How was he?"

"Better."

"Did you go back in the afternoon?"

What was he, some sort of errand boy for the Sisters of Charity?

"I didn't have time."

"Promise you'll go tomorrow?"

The woman was obsessed!

"I promise."

The last thing he needed was the hassle of having to go and help a vagabond who had no desire to have people about trying to help him!

He didn't sleep too well.

He woke up several times, always with the same question in his head: What had Giovanna wanted to know? He was certain that she'd given him the answer without wanting to, but he couldn't figure out what it was.

As soon as he got to the office he called Fazio.

"Did you draft a report of Arturo Barletta's declarations?"

"Yessir. I've got it in my office."

"Go and see what time he says he got to his father's beach house that morning."

Fazio went out and then came back.

"Eight o'clock."

"And do you remember at what time his sister Giovanna said he called her in Montelusa to tell her their father had been murdered?"

Fazio gave him a confused look, then slapped himself in the forehead.

"See? You're getting old yourself!" said Montalbano. "Yesterday evening Giovanna, whom I ran into by chance, reconfirmed that Arturo called her at seven-thirty."

"Who knows how long Arturo had already been at the house!" Fazio exclaimed.

"At any rate, he didn't get there before six."

"Why do you say that?"

"Because Pasquano claims that's more or less when Barletta died of poisoning."

"I'm sorry, but if he was poisoned at six, Arturo must have gotten there a few minutes earlier."

"But if things went the way I think they went, it wasn't Arturo who poisoned his father."

"It wasn't?"

"No. He was the one who shot him, thinking he was still drinking his morning coffee."

"We would have to prove that."

"Right."

"Shall I call him in?"

"Wait. So you call him in and then what? You politely ask him whether he killed his father? No, we have to find another way. What was his wife's name?"

"Michela Lollo."

"Go and pick her up. And bring her here to me before she has time to talk to her husband."

Fazio dashed out faster than a lightning bolt.

"Did you read the letters?" Mimì asked when he came in.

"Only about ten lines in the first one."

"Hurry up and finish them so we can talk."

"Do they seem so important to you?"

"That's the feeling I get."

"Listen, Mimì; Fazio and I discovered something."

And he told him about the two different versions of Arturo's time of arrival at the house, about his pressing need for money, and about how important the will was for him.

"So we finally have something to work with," was Augello's comment.

"Yeah, but it's still not much. I want to question Arturo's wife. You need to try to find out at what time that Sunday morning Arturo left his place in Montelusa to drive out to the country house."

"That won't be easy."

"Well, in the meantime find out what kind of car he has, the year, and the license plate number. And where he normally keeps it. In a garage? Outside his apartment building?"

"Salvo, don't forget it was a Sunday."

"So what?"

"It means the stores were all closed and so there'll be a lot fewer potential witnesses."

"We'll take what we can get, Mimì. I can only wish you luck."

· · ·

. . . and fused in a sort of vibrant inevitability, the same that has overwhelmed us for so many years.

But, perhaps because of all that time too long apart, the last meeting was wonderfully more intense.

I came out of your embrace with a wholly new sensation, which at that moment I was unable to explain to myself.

It was a combination of happiness and fear.

Now, at two months' distance, I've found the reason for the fear.

I am pregnant.

I have proof of this, having taken a test.

I am carrying your baby inside me.

You should know in fact that I am no longer sleeping with him. I don't think I could stand it.

But the fear has vanished. It has changed into an extraordinary, growing happiness.

You should know that I am unwilling to give up this child of ours. Not for all the money in the world.

I can already anticipate your objections.

With him, however, I know how to act. As naturally as possible. Tonight I will clench my teeth and give in to his insistent demands.

Nobody will suspect that the child is ours, neither he nor those around us.

You will carry on your life of love affairs with those young girls I'm so jealous of, a life I am forced to accept because I can do nothing to prevent it.

I will continue to play the part of the faithful companion.

There was a time in our lives when we met almost daily, despite the extreme risks. Then we had to slow things down for a variety of reasons I needn't go into here.

You know them as well as I do.

Well, I wanted to tell you I no longer wish for those days when it was easier for us to meet.

I don't wish for them because now you are inside me at every hour of the day and night, through the creature that is growing inside me.

Perhaps only another woman could understand me.

See you soon, I hope.

He picked up a pen and underlined a few words he wanted to discuss with Augello.

At that moment Fazio appeared.

"She's here with me. Shall I have her come in?"

"Where was she?"

"At home."

"Was her husband around?"

"No, he was out."

"Bring her in."

Michela, too, as a woman, was no joke. But compared to Giovanna, who was truly elegant, she, though wearing what must have been rather expensive clothing, was only striking and a little coarse. She, too, was blonde. How many blondes were there in Vigàta anyway?

She seemed to be in a combative mood, and indeed she immediately went on the attack:

"What is this? How dare you! A woman can't sit at home minding her own business without having a cop come in and tell her she has to come with him? Where are we anyway? Africa?"

"Please sit down, signora."

"No! I'll remain standing because in five minutes I'm leaving! And I warn you: I'm going to talk to my lawyer about this!"

"Signora, if you'll just answer a few questions I'll let you go right away, and nobody, not even your husband, will know you've been here. Otherwise I'll be forced to summon you officially, with all the publicity that usually accompanies cases like this. Is that clear? So, the less time we waste, the better it is for all of us. Please sit down."

Michela, still furious, sat down at the edge of the chair.

Montalbano decided to use the rapid-fire questions strategy with her. That would tame her pretty quickly.

"I don't understand why you made me come here. I don't know anything about anything—"

"I don't doubt that."

"Then why—"

"Do you have any children?"

"No."

"Why not?"

For the first time, Michela seemed a little confused.

"Well, when we first got married I wasn't . . . then we . . ."

"I'm sorry, inappropriate question. Do you work?"

"No."

"Have you ever had a job?"

"Yes. When I was eighteen I—"

"Never mind. What level of school did you complete?"

"Junior high."

"Give me one of your teachers' names."

"Genuardi."

"What did he teach?"

"Italian."

"Good, good. Just one minute."

Montalbano randomly grabbed a sheet of paper off the top of his desk, read it very slowly, twisting his mouth up variously with concentration and self-satisfaction. Michela took an embroidered handkerchief out of her purse and held it in both hands. The inspector set the sheet of paper down, looked at it pensively, then resumed.

"Does your father work?"

"He's retired."

"What did he do for a living?"

"Night security guard."

"What about your mother?"

"She doesn't work eith—"

"What did she do before?"

"She . . . cleaned apartments."

Michela felt embarrassed to say her mother had been a cleaning lady.

"Do you have any brothers or sisters?"

"A brother who—"

"What's his name?"

"Giaco—"

"Do you have a car?"

"Yes, a Fiat Pa—"

"What about your husband?"

"What?"

"Your husband. Does he have a car?"

"Yes, a—"

"How many cars do you have in the family?"

"T-two—"

"And before?"

"Before what?"

"Before marrying Arturo Barletta?"

Michela was now clearly bewildered. Her combative stance was almost completely gone. She couldn't figure out where Montalbano was going with all this.

"Could you . . . repeat the question?"

"Did you have one?"

"Did I have one what?"

"Aren't we talking about a car?"

"Oh! Yes. I had a—"

"How old?"

"I couldn't say."

"I mean you."

"Me? I was twenty."

"So it was a used car?"

"Yes."

"But it worked well?"

"Uh . . . pretty well."

"Let's talk about something else."

He grabbed the sheet of paper again, cast a quick glance at it, hummed with his mouth closed, then set it down.

"What time did you wake up on the morning your father-in-law was killed?"

"At . . . let me think . . ."

"What time do you usually wake up?"

"At nine."

"How did you find out?"

"Find out what?"

"That your father-in-law had been murdered."

"My sister-in-law Giovanna called."

"Not your husband?"

"No."

"What time was it?"

"It might have been . . . it wasn't yet eight o'clock."

"At what time did your husband go out?"

"I don't know, I was asleep."

"Even when you're asleep you usually notice when the person beside you gets up or moves . . . You didn't notice anything?"

"The past two nights . . ."

"The past two nights?"

"He . . . had trouble sleeping. He'd get up, get back in bed . . . So I couldn't really tell you if . . ."

"Did you ask him why he was so agitated?"

"No."

"Why not?"

"We were going through a—"

"Had you quarreled?"

"Yes."

"And you weren't speaking?"

"No."

"What did you quarrel about?"

"Per-personal things."

"I see. Do you have any idea?"

"Of what?"

"Of why your husband was agitated."

"Well . . . the company he works for is . . . He has a lot of debts and . . ."

"Why didn't you go too?"

"Go . . . where?"

"To your father-in-law's house, with your husband."

"Because I had . . . stuff to do at home."

By this point the woman's brain was smoking. Nevertheless, she bucked up and said:

"Inspector, I really don't understand why—"

"You will. Any female friends?"

"Who?"

"You."

"A few."

"One in particular?"

"My sister-in-law Giovanna."

"Do you often go out together?"

"Fairly often."

"Where do you go?"

"Uh . . . I dunno, the movies . . . or to—"

"Your first car, the one you got when you were twenty, was it a gift from the late Cosimo Barletta, who was your lover?"

She hadn't been expecting this. Montalbano had led her very far afield.

She gave such a start in her chair that she practically fell off. She turned pale as a corpse and started panting as she spoke, as if out of breath.

"He . . . he . . . was never . . . my . . . I . . . it was Arturo who . . . introduced me to him."

"We have photos."

It was a whopping lie, but it achieved the desired effect. Michela's eyes opened wide, and she got a sort of tic in her left eyelid.

"What . . . what photos?"

"Of you and Cosimo Barletta as you're . . . know what I mean? Didn't you know he had that nice little habit? Didn't your friend Giovanna tell you? Fazio, show the lady a few pictures."

It was a dangerous bluff. Fazio got up and went over to the filing cabinet.

At the same time Michela sprang to her feet, put her hands over her eyes, and cried:

"I don't want to see them!"

"Okay, fine. Sit down."

She obeyed like a puppet.

"How long were you his mistress?"

"Four months."

"When did Arturo fall in love with you?"

"From the start."

"Meaning?"

"After I'd been with . . . for a week . . . he came to the house unannounced . . . I was on my way out and . . ."

"Where would you and Arturo meet?"

"When I worked as a secretary for the engineer Porzio, Arturo would wait for me outside when I got off work."

"Did Barletta make a fuss when Arturo told him he wanted to marry you?"

"No."

"Why not?"

"Because he was already tired of me . . . I realized."

15

At this point Michela was no longer in any
condition to refuse to answer the inspector's
questions. The decisive round was beginning, but
Montalbano intended to pull his punches a little.

"And you?"

"And me what?"

"Had you grown tired of him too?"

"For me there was nothing to get tired of or
not to get tired of. I had no feelings for him. He
wanted my body, I gave it to him, he would do
what he wanted and then he would pay me. I felt
a little ashamed, yes. Not in front of him, but
sometimes, when I was by myself . . . He was . . .
generous."

"Listen, what were the circumstances that time
your father-in-law put his hands on you?"

Her handkerchief by now had become a
dark little ball drenched in sweat. She looked
surprised.

"How did you fi—"

"Please answer the question."

"One day . . . at the beach house."

"How did it happen?"

"Is it really necess—"

"Yes."

She heaved a big sigh before starting.

"Everyone had gone down to the beach, and I was alone in the house, in the kitchen, making salad . . . I didn't hear him come in . . . He pushed me facedown on the table with one hand and held me there—he was a very strong man—and with the other hand he pulled up my skirt . . . I got so angry . . . But I couldn't yell because the others might hear. I'd thought that affair was over and done with, but instead . . . at that point . . ."

"Your husband intervened."

"Him?!"

"It wasn't Arturo who intervened?"

"It was, but not . . . Is that what he told you?"

"Don't ask any questions."

"I noticed there was a knife on the table . . . I grabbed it and . . . I don't know how I managed to turn around . . . I jabbed at him with the knife but he blocked it with his left hand . . . and at that moment Arturo came in and disarmed me . . . His father slapped me twice so hard it nearly knocked my head off, and then ran out . . ."

"What did your husband say to you?"

"Nothing."

"Fine, but what happened afterwards?"

She blushed.

"Afterwards . . . Arturo took me into our bedroom and wanted . . . he was very aroused. I'm positive he . . . In fact he later confessed to me that he'd been watching us for a few minutes, there in the kitchen. I don't think . . ."

"Go on."

"I don't think he would have intervened if I hadn't resisted . . . He would have let it all happen."

"Why?"

"Because he would never oppose his father."

"But does Arturo love you?"

She thought about this for a moment before answering.

"I don't know . . . I think so. He still . . . desires me, that's true, as in the days . . . but in front of his father . . ."

"So it was you who no longer wanted to see Cosimo Barletta?"

"That's right."

"What did you and your husband quarrel about?"

"I would rather . . ."

At this point all that was left to do was to deliver the knockout punch.

"Signora, before we go any further, it is my duty to tell you that you're suspected of murder."

"I am?!"

"Three strands of blond hair were found in Barletta's bed. We've been told they may be yours. Afterwards you'll have to give us a hair sample for testing."

Michela made a sincerely astonished face.

"But that hair can't be mine!"

"Let me finish. For your own good, tell me the

truth: How long ago did you resume your affair with your father-in-law?"

Michela's face transformed and she leapt to her feet like a Fury. She was shaking all over with rage. All her ladylike composure was gone.

"Who fed you *that* bullshit, eh? Who? I hadn't seen Barletta for years! For years! Ever since that time at the house! Not even at Christmas! He was as good as dead to me! And then my fucking cheesedick of a husband suddenly wanted me . . . to go back with his father at least once! He wanted me to start fucking him again!"

"He wanted you to resume your relationship with his father?"

"Yes!"

"And that was why you quarreled?"

"Yes!"

"When did he ask you to do this?"

"Three days before the pig was murdered! He was insistent! 'What's it to you?' he would say. 'When it's done we'll be better off. Don't you see? If you go along, my father will change the will, which is now all in Giovanna's favor.' But I refused! By now it makes me puke just to think of the goddamned pig! I'm not some kind of whore, after all!"

She started crying.

"Okay, that's enough. Take the lady home," Montalbano said to Fazio.

Then, turning to Michela:

"I beg you please to forgive me."

"Will you wait for me? I'll be right back," said Fazio.

"No. We can talk this afternoon."

At Enzo's he ate very little. What Michela had just recounted had squelched his appetite, though he took his customary stroll along the jetty just the same.

Sitting down on the flat rock, he started extracting the gist from the words he'd heard. And the gist was that Michela's entire deposition had been an involuntary indictment of her husband.

True, she hadn't been able to say at what time Arturo got up that morning, but she'd revealed something of great importance: that her husband had become a desperate man.

Probably the loan sharks he'd resorted to had threatened to kill him if he didn't pay up.

It's possible they believed that Arturo could turn to his father for help. But that wasn't the case. Barletta didn't give a flying fuck about his son's troubles.

Unless . . .

In fact the idea of bringing Michela to him, ready to jump into bed, wasn't a bad one. Had she agreed to it, Arturo would have been in a position to ask his father for the money he needed. She was the only commodity of exchange he had available.

Wait a second, Montalbà.

Wasn't there a huge contradiction in Arturo's behavior? If he was buried in debt, it seemed primarily because his wife had him spending all kinds of money and he was afraid that if he didn't give in, she might take on a rich lover the way her friend Giovanna had done.

But if he loved Michela that much, then how could he stand the fact that another man . . .

No, wrong. Michela was quite clear on this point when she talked about Arturo having a genuine physical infatuation with her.

The word *love* was not applicable.

Okay, but if someone desires another's body to that degree, how can he surrender that body to someone else?

Use your brain, Montalbà! This "someone else" is not just some stranger, but the guy's father!

And his master! Didn't Michela herself say, in all sincerity, that Arturo would have been capable of watching the rape happen without intervening because it involved his father?

But Michela had firmly rejected her husband's proposal. And he'd insisted, because that was to be his last desperate attempt before he was forced to take the terrible, final, definitive step . . .

Yes, that must be how it had gone.

• • •

Back at the station, he related to Fazio what he'd been thinking, and Fazio came out in complete agreement.

"When you got back to Michela's house, was her husband there?"

"No, he hadn't returned yet."

"Do you think she'll tell him what she told us?"

"I don't think she'll even tell him she came here. At least that's what she led me to believe."

"So Arturo still doesn't know we've got him in our sights?"

"I really don't think so."

Montalbano sat there thinking for a moment. Then he started laughing.

"Care to let me in on the joke?" said Fazio.

"Can you tell me exactly what we will have achieved by arresting Arturo?"

Fazio looked perplexed.

"What do you mean, 'what we will have achieved'? We will have arrested the killer!"

"You call someone who shoots a man already dead a killer?"

"His intention was to kill his father. The fact that the guy was already dead is irrelevant to me."

"Fazio, you'll see at the trial whether it's relevant or not! But the real problem is that we haven't the slightest idea who the woman was that killed him!"

"So for you it was definitely a woman?"

"I'm ninety-nine percent certain. It was the one who'd slept with him that last night."

"Then why let the whole night go by?"

"Maybe because she didn't have an opportunity to use the poison before then. Say they went out to a restaurant for dinner. How's she gonna poison his dishes with all those people around? And apparently Barletta didn't get thirsty at night; in fact there was no water glass on his bedside table. The murderess had no choice but to wait until the next morning's coffee."

"But why did they wake up so early?"

"There must be an explanation. Maybe she told him she could spend the night with him at the house but had to be back at home by seven in the morning at the latest."

Fazio seemed satisfied with this.

"Chief, here's a question just for the sake of argument: If Michela had agreed to do what her husband wanted, are you so sure Barletta would, in the end, have helped his son? I don't think so. He would have enjoyed Arturo's wife and then let his son stew in his own juices."

"I agree," said Montalbano.

Mimì Augello came back to the office around six that evening. He looked pleased. He must have discovered something good.

"Call Fazio," he said to Montalbano as he sat himself down. "That'll spare me having to say the same thing twice."

Fazio showed up at once.

"I got really lucky," Augello began. "Remember when I said that, being Sunday morning, the stores would be all closed and therefore there would be no witnesses?"

"Yes."

"I was wrong."

"They were open?" asked Fazio.

"No, all closed. Except one. A bookshop directly opposite the front door of Arturo Barletta's building."

"Why was it open?"

"They were doing inventory."

"They saw him go out?"

"No."

"What, then?"

"The bookstore's owner, whose name is Varvaro, was familiar with the car that Arturo usually parked outside his front door. Varvaro arrived at the store with an employee at six a.m. that Sunday morning. And Arturo's car was there. They went in and rolled the shutter back down. Five minutes later, Varvaro realized he'd forgotten his cigarettes in the car. So he reopened the shutter, went out, and noticed that Arturo's car was no longer there."

"And it takes about half an hour to drive

from Montelusa to the beach house," Fazio commented.

"For me it's not enough," said Montalbano.

"Why not?" asked Fazio.

"Because Arturo can always maintain that he had to do something else before going to his father's house. Or that the car broke down or something similar. And that was why he got to the house at eight."

Mimì Augello smiled.

"But didn't I tell you guys I got *really* lucky? I found another witness. Signor Modica."

"And who's he?"

"The owner of a house about a quarter mile past Barletta's beach house, down the same road. I thought I should go and talk to him. He told me where he lives in town, and I met with him there. He said that on that Sunday morning he was on his way to his house when another car passed him aggressively, running him off the road and not stopping to assist. It was Arturo's car."

"Does he remember what time it was?"

"Yes. It was probably around six-thirty-five, six-forty. Modica's wife hurt her forehead. When Modica got to his house, he gave his wife first aid then got back in his car in a rage and drove to Barletta's house. When he pulled up and got out, he saw Arturo come running to him all upset, yelling: 'Papa's been shot! Go away!' Modica got scared, put the car in gear, and drove off. Is that enough for you?"

"So he's certain Arturo was chasing him away?" asked Montalbano.

"Absolutely."

"So Arturo behaved in an unnatural way. Because someone who's just found his father shot dead isn't going to send people away. If anything, he's going to ask the first person he sees for help. Whereas Arturo doesn't want any outsiders in his hair. He wants both hands free to look for the will. It's all pretty clear," the inspector concluded.

"So what now?" asked Augello.

"Now I have to go and talk to Tommaseo. Congratulations, Mimì, not just on your luck, but on your police work. Well done."

As he was entering the prosecutor's office, Montalbano stopped dead in his tracks.

Standing on a chair, Tommaseo was attaching enlargements of Barletta's photographs to the wall with thumbtacks. One wall was already entirely covered. On the desk lay another fifty or so photographic enlargements. The room looked like the editorial office of a pornographic magazine.

"You really ought to put a sign on the door saying 'Minors forbidden to enter,' don't you think?" Montalbano joked.

But Tommaseo took him seriously.

"You may be right," he said, climbing down from the chair.

He looked around and seemed satisfied.

"I had them enlarged so you could see the details better."

On the desk there was even a magnifying glass worthy of Sherlock Holmes. Montalbano figured that Tommaseo, forever fixated on fantasies of women, must be spending tortured nights in bed turning the images of the exhibition he'd mounted over and over in his head.

"Have you identified any of them?"

"Four, so far. Inspector Mazzacolla is doing a remarkable job."

The inspector noticed that the prosecutor's face looked waxen and bloodless, and his hands were trembling slightly. Surely he was on the verge of collapse.

"Have you interrogated them?"

"Oh, yes, oh, yes! At length! I've penetrated their innermost depths!"

He felt around in his pocket and took out a small box, which he opened, extracting a pill that he then swallowed, drinking it down with half a glass of water he had within reach.

This stuff's gonna kill the poor guy, thought Montalbano.

"And have you come up with anything?"

"Bah . . . These arc girls who lie without

hesitation, you know . . . One says she was with Barletta only once because he got her drunk . . . Another says she was forced to give in . . . The fact of the matter is that Barletta had a solid argument for persuading them to go to bed with him: money. And he didn't skimp on them, either. Just think, the last one he was with—"

"You've discovered who Barletta's last girl-friend was?"

"Yes. Didn't Inspector Mazzacolla tell you? It's that one there, see?"

He pointed to one of the photos posted on the wall. A girl who must not even have been twenty—gorgeous, portrayed completely nude from behind, with her head turned to look at the photographer.

"As you can see," Tommaseo continued, "she's a brunette. So she couldn't have been the girl from Barletta's last night. She also has an unassailable alibi."

"How long had she been going with Barletta?"

"For a month. And he claimed to be madly in love with her! Imagine that! She even said—though it's clearly a lie—that Barletta had solemnly sworn to her that he would make out his will in her favor and show it to her the next time they met, on the following Monday. But he was murdered on Sunday."

Montalbano felt a violent electrical shock run

through his entire body. He managed to control himself. Then he started laughing.

"That's the most absurd thing I've heard so far about Barletta! But, just out of curiosity, what's her name?"

"The girl's? Alina Camera. She's from Vigàta. But what did you come here to tell me?"

"Nothing. I was just passing by and came to say hello."

"Well, thanks. How's your slice of the investigation going?"

"We suspect the son, Arturo—but it's only a hunch, mind you."

"Really? And why would he have killed his father?"

"Because the father was preying on his wife."

"The man didn't spare anyone!" Tommaseo exclaimed, slightly envious. "So he wanted to . . . even with his daughter-in-law?"

"So it seems."

"Is she attractive?" Tommaseo asked, licking his lips.

But weren't all the girls he had around him, even if only in photographs, enough for him? He had to sidetrack the guy. That was all the wretched Michela needed, to have the public prosecutor all over her!

"Well, that's the strange thing."

"What is?"

"She's pretty plain, that's what. Slightly bow-legged, a little hint of a mustache . . . Who knows what he saw in her."

Tommaseo seemed disappointed.

"Bah! When it comes to sex, man is inscrutable!" he said philosophically.

Montalbano concurred, nodding in understanding. Then he asked:

"Do you want to interview her yourself?"

Tommaseo didn't seem too enthusiastic.

"No, no . . . That's your slice of the investigation, anyway. Well . . ."

He stood up and held out his hand. Which was sweaty. He was anxious to get back to studying those photos with his magnifying glass.

Once outside, the inspector checked his watch. Ten past eight exactly. If they didn't waste any time, he and the others might just manage. He called Catarella.

"Yer orders, Chief!"

"Are Augello and Fazio still there?"

"Yessir, Chief, 'ey're still onna premisses."

"Tell them to wait for me. I'm on my way. Meantime pass me Fazio."

"What is it, Chief?"

"Fazio, write this name down: Alina Camera. She's a girl of about twenty, from Vigàta. If possible, bring her to my office. Even if it's impossible."

"Right now?"

"Right now."

"Did Prosecutor Tommaseo sign an arrest warrant?"

"No."

"Why not?"

"Because I didn't ask him to. It seemed better to hear first what this girl has to say. Don't waste any time. Find me Alina."

"She's here," Fazio said to the inspector as he entered the station.

"Alina?"

"That's right."

"Well done! How did you manage?"

"I got the idea to look her up in the phone book. There she was: first name, last name, and address. I got lucky too, just like Inspector Augello, because when I got there she was on her way to the movies with a girlfriend."

"What was her reaction?"

"As if I'd invited her for a cup of coffee. She said good-bye to her friend and didn't make a peep of protest the whole way here in the car."

"Bring her into my office, and you and Augello come too."

16

In person, Alina Camera was even better than in the photograph. Mimì, gazing at her, looked spellbound by her beauty. You certainly couldn't say that Barletta didn't know how to pick his women. But how was it that when Barletta walked about town he was able to flush out all these beautiful girls, whereas he, the inspector, never saw a single one? Maybe Barletta was endowed with an eye for it, like a dog with a nose for truffles.

"Please sit down. I'll keep you only a few minutes."

"Okay."

She was completely indifferent, as Fazio had said. Actually, she seemed a little bored.

"Do you work?"

"No. I'll be studying modern literature in Palermo. I just enrolled, a little over a week ago."

"Do you live alone?"

"Yes."

"And your parents?"

"They live here, in Vigàta."

"Do you rent the apartment you live in?"

"No. It's mine."

"Did your parents buy it for you?"

"My parents? They barely have enough money to make it to the end of the month."

"Then how . . ."

"Cosimo bought it for me, two months ago."

And who was that? She saw the question in the inspector's eyes.

"Barletta," she explained.

Right. His first name was Cosimo. She felt the need to add:

"I've already said that to Inspector Mazzacolla and Dr. Tommaseo—that he bought me the apartment."

"Were you already his mistress?"

"No."

"Then why did he buy you an apartment?"

"To persuade me to go with him."

"Were you persuaded?"

"Yes. The same day he gave me the keys."

"I see. Listen, it's late, so I'll get straight to the point. Is it true that Barletta fell in love with you?"

"Yes."

"He never did with any of his other girls; why with you?"

"Maybe because, unlike the other girls, I resisted his advances for three months before I . . . I have letters from him in which it's clear . . ."

Now this was news!

"He wrote you letters?"

"Yes, about ten or so. They're funny."

"Why?"

"An old man writing love letters, like a little boy . . . And the grammar's terrible . . ."

Though she was indeed speaking, it was as though she had no part in the words she was saying. She wasn't really a girl of flesh and blood, but a sort of refrigerator.

"Did you talk about these letters with Prosecutor Tommaseo?"

"No."

"You should have. Why didn't you?"

"Because when I told them that Cosimo was in love with me, they started laughing and didn't believe it. So . . ."

"Where are they?"

"The letters? At my place."

"Would you have any problem with us reading them?"

"I couldn't care less."

"What were the circumstances when Barletta told you he would change the will in your favor?"

Fazio and Augello, who knew nothing about this detail, pricked up their astonished ears.

"The second time he came to see me, I told him that twice was quite enough for me and I no longer wanted to . . . that he could even take back the apartment. He started crying. He wrote me a desperate letter . . . It's with the others . . . I let him come back, on the condition that he pay for my studies. He deposited a large sum in the bank in my name, enough to get me to graduation. I want to study, but my parents aren't in a position to support me . . . And so, it was either him or someone else . . . Since then, he's wanted me almost every day."

"When was the last time you saw him?"

"It was a Thursday. That was when he told me that he would change the will in my favor, on the condition that I wouldn't leave him till he died. He said he would show it to me the next time we met, which would have been the following Monday. He specified that it would be a proper will, drawn up with a notary, and that he wasn't kidding. But he was killed on Sunday."

She told the story without any alteration in her tone of voice, without once showing any emotion—whether shame, displeasure, resentment, or sorrow. Nothing.

"Why did you not see him after Thursday?"

"I went to Palermo on Friday morning because the university had opened for registration. A girlfriend of mine had agreed to put me up for two days. And in fact I came back to Vigàta on Sunday evening. I only found out from the TV that Cosimo had been killed. Inspector Mazzacolla has checked all this out."

Montalbano, Augello, and Fazio all exchanged a quick glance. There was nothing else to discuss.

"All right, then, thanks. You can go. Fazio,

please give the young lady a ride home and have her give you the letters."

"Good-bye," said Alina.

She stood up, adjusted her skirt, and went out as indifferently as she had come in.

"You know what?" said Mimì the moment the two were alone in the room. "That girl scares me."

"Me too," Montalbano concurred.

"Good thing she has an alibi, because that kid would be fully capable of killing a man without a second thought."

"I think I understand why Barletta fell in love with her."

"Why?"

"Because she was just like him. Totally devoid of humanity."

It took Fazio less than half an hour to go and come back. He dropped a packet of letters on the desk.

"Can I say something?" he said. "That girl . . ."

"Scared you?" said Montalbano and Augello in unison.

"You too?"

"What Alina told us," said the inspector, "helps us understand at least two things. The first is that Arturo was aware of his father's intention to change the will. Something that he had always feared—that his father would fall in love with some girl and do something really stupid—was actually happening. He'd talked about it with Giovanna. Changing the will meant that he would lose even the lesser part of the inheritance, since the greater part would go to his sister. In short, he wouldn't see a cent. The second thing is that we finally have the answer to a question that has long been swirling in my brain: What was it that Barletta absolutely had to be prevented from doing on that Sunday? The answer: changing the will. Sunday was the last possible day; Monday would have been too late, since Barletta had promised Alina he would let her read it that day. Is that much clear?"

"Quite," said Augello.

Montalbano glanced at his watch. It was half past nine.

"Now, let's look for a final confirmation. Fazio, do you remember the name of Barletta's notary friend, the one Giovanna mentioned to us?"

"Piscopo, I think she said. He's in Montelusa."

"Look him up in the phone book and ask him if we can come and pay him a visit."

"At this hour?"

"You bet your life, at this hour. Explain to him that we have no choice. All three of us will go."

"I'm gonna go call Beba and tell her I'll be home late," said Mimì, getting up and going out.

Fazio returned about ten minutes later.

"He made something of a fuss, but in the end he gave in. He'll be waiting for us at his place."

• • •

They left in a squad car with Fazio at the wheel. When they drew near the street the notary lived on, Montalbano said:

"Turn the siren on."

"Why?"

"For psychological effect. The notary has to think this is something very serious. That'll lessen his resistance to our questions."

The notary himself answered the door.

He was a distinguished man of about sixty, well dressed with gold-rimmed glasses.

"I heard you arrive. Please come in."

"Mr. Piscopo, I'm Inspector Montalbano."

He then introduced Augello and Fazio. They were shown into a sitting room with fine furnishings.

"I wish I could offer you something, but I'm not sure I have anything . . . I'm a bachelor and I live alone. I mostly come here just to sleep."

"Please don't trouble yourself. I thank you for being so kind as to receive us, and I apologize for the hour. I'll take as little of your time as possible. Was Cosimo Barletta a friend of yours?"

"Yes."

"And did he file his last will and testament with you?"

"No."

"So he wasn't a client of yours. But as a friend,

did he ask you for advice on how to draw up a holographic will?"

"Yes."

"So, as a friend, you're not held to any code of professional secrecy."

"Well . . ."

"I just want to know whether he made one or not."

"He did."

"And Giovanna, Barletta's daughter . . . do you know her?"

The notary gave a hint of a smile before answering.

"Pretty well."

"Giovanna told me that the will favored her over her brother Arturo. Because she had children and Arturo didn't. Is that correct?"

"Yes."

"Did Barletta later express to you any intention to annul this will?"

"Yes."

"And to change it to favor someone outside the family?"

"Yes."

"With both children left completely out of the will?"

"As he intended it, yes. He might have left a small sum for Giovanna. But, you see . . ."

"Go on."

"A testament of the sort that Cosimo had in

mind isn't so easy to draw up. There are not only problems of legitimacy . . . it's too easily contested . . . it can be challenged if every possible exception isn't anticipated . . . In short, I offered to lend him a hand, as I'd done with the first will."

"Did he accept?"

"Yes. He called me on Friday morning—I remember it well—to invite me to come and spend Sunday with him at his house."

"Did he tell you that Arturo would also be there?"

"Arturo? His presence would have been inconvenient, to say the least. He would have had to witness the drafting of a will that was going to disinherit him! No, Cosimo stated explicitly that it would be just the two of us."

"When did you learn that your friend had been murdered?"

"That same Sunday, at around eight-thirty in the morning."

"Who told you?"

"Giovanna called. It was a terrible blow for me. I was just on my way to see him."

Montalbano stood up, and Augello and Fazio did likewise.

"I thank you for your courtesy and cooperation, sir," said Montalbano, shaking his hand.

"So what now?" asked Fazio as they were driving back to Vigàta.

"Now you're going to take me home. I want Arturo in front of me at nine o'clock tomorrow morning. Mimì, you pass by the office and get Barletta's letters to Alina. I want you to read them tonight and—"

"Why always me?"

"Because I still have to finish reading the other ones, from the unknown woman."

His home telephone lately was in the habit of starting to ring every time he was unlocking the front door. Fortunately he picked it up in time.

"Where were you? This is the second time I've called," said Livia.

"I was just coming home."

"Did you go and see Mario?"

Good God, this was becoming an obsession!

"Believe me, I didn't have a free moment . . ."

"You never have a free moment to do the things I ask you to do!"

"Don't put it that way!"

"Then how should I put it?"

"That I absolutely had no time, period. I didn't refrain from going just to spite you."

"I wish I could believe you, but . . ."

They were off to a very bad start.

They squabbled for about ten minutes, then, to conclude, Montalbano swore to her that he would go and visit the vagabond the following day.

Adelina had made him fried pasta with broccoli and a salad of calamari rings, shrimp, celery, carrots, and passuluna olives. As he was heating the pasta in the oven, he set the table outside on the veranda.

When he'd finished, he cleared the table, grabbed his cigarettes and lighter, and sat back down outside. He stuck a hand in his jacket pocket, took out the letters, and started reading them.

> You're pigheaded. You never give up until everyone, like it or not, submits to your desires. This time, however, I will stand up to you.
>
> You will never make me change my mind. I've told you this in writing and in person.
>
> And I'll say it again: I will not get an abortion.
>
> We shall be forever bound by this creature, even more than we are by the secret that we've been harboring deep in our hearts for years.
>
> We made a lightning decision that terrible day. Do you remember?
>
> Without saying a word, without exchanging a glance, we acted in unison and let things take their course.

242

Now, however, you do not agree with me.
And this pains me.
But my mind is made up.
I shall make my own choice—for both of us.

He took a look at the other letters. In one she talked about a trip they had taken together; in another she thanked him for the presents he'd lavished on her and the money he was continually giving her; in a third she reproached him for his continual affairs with other women and declared that she would get her revenge by paying him back "in kind" . . . The last letter particularly struck him.

In it she remembered when she was a little girl and Barletta took her to the circus . . .

This was an important clue. It meant that Barletta had known her—the woman who would one day become his mistress and the mother of his child—when she was still a little girl. She must have been the daughter of a close friend of his.

But, apart from this last letter, there was nothing in the others that might help to identify the woman who wrote them.

He went inside, closed the French door, and got into bed.

For some reason, those letters had made him uneasy.

"Fazio, before bringing Arturo in, I want to tell you that I absolutely need you to inform yourself as to who Barletta's friends were, what people used to come to his house, and so on. You can start on it this afternoon. I'm gonna go now."

"What?" said a shocked Mimì. "And what about interrogating Arturo?"

"You guys can take care of it."

"Excuse me, Salvo, but—"

"Mimì, the man killed his father over a question of money. It's the basest motive conceivable. On top of that, he killed him in the stupidest fashion imaginable, letting himself be seen by the neighbor like that, calling his sister at seven-thirty and telling us that it was eight when we know he was already at the house before seven, and shooting his father without realizing the guy was already dead! Why should I waste an hour of my life interrogating a moron like that? Tell him about the witnesses—the bookseller, the neighbor—and tell him what the notary and his wife Michela told us. The guy'll crack, you'll see."

"And what if he wants a lawyer?"

"You'll get him one. Then you'll handcuff him and take him to Tommaseo. And since I think this business will keep you busy all morning, we'll meet back up after lunch."

244

He went out, got in his car, and sped home to Marinella.

"What happened?" asked Adelina, taken by surprise when he charged in at an unusual time of day.

"Nothing, nothing."

He took off his clothes, put on his bathing suit, ran down to the beach, and threw himself into the sea.

Merely talking about Arturo had made him feel dirty all over.

Seeing his face might well have made him vomit.

The water was cold, but it washed him clean.

He went back into the house, grabbed the unknown woman's letters, and took them out on the veranda.

"Could you make me some coffee, Adelì?"

"Comin' a right uppa, sir."

There was something in those letters that made him suspicious, but he couldn't bring it into focus.

". . . the same that *has overwhelmed us for so many years . . .*"

". . . because of *all that time too long apart . . .*"

". . . nobody will suspect that the child is ours, *neither he nor those around us . . .*"

". . . a time in our lives *when we met almost daily, despite the extreme risks . . .*"

What were these extreme risks? Apparently it was risky not only for her, but for Barletta as well.

But normally Barletta didn't give a flying fuck about the risks his lusts created for him! One needed only to look at the way he behaved with Michela, having tried to rape her in the kitchen while the rest of the family was on the beach, within shouting distance!

So what was it about their meetings that made them so dangerous?

"You' caffee, Isspecter."

He went over the letters for an hour but got nowhere.

"Why dona you stay anna eat atta home, issead a allway goin' out to the restaurant! 'Oo knows wha' kinda 'sgustin' stuff 'ey givvin' you ta eat! Oil 'ass fried anna riffried, sauce 'assa gonna bad, rottid fish . . ."

One ate magnificently well at Enzo's, but Adelina was convinced she was the best house-keeper and cook in the world.

"What will you make for me?"

"I mekka li'l pasta 'ncasciata."

He managed to control himself—otherwise he would have hugged her, kissed her, and danced a waltz with her.

"And you'll also make something for this evening?"

"O' course!"

Adelina set the table on the veranda, and he had a feast. Not so much owing to the dish his housekeeper had cooked—which was always the quintessence of heaven—but because that meal came with the best seasoning one could ever hope for: a day of sun, with an ever-so-light breeze that not only was not a disturbance, but also carried the scent of the sea.

Instead of taking his walk out to the end of the jetty, he strolled along the beach, barefoot, with the water every so often caressing his feet.

By the time he got back to the office, it was three o'clock. In the main entrance he ran into Fazio, who was on his way out.

"Where are you off to?"

"To do what you asked me to do this morning. Look for close friends of Barletta's . . ."

"Is Augello in?"

"Yessir."

"Then stay here. Go and get him, then both of you come to my office."

17

"Tell me how it went this morning," he said, as soon as both of his men had sat down in front of him.

"How would you expect?" said Mimì. "When I read him all the charges he turned as white as a corpse, and the only thing he said in the end was that he wanted his lawyer. But his lawyer wasn't available, so we took Arturo to see Tommaseo, whom Fazio had called to let him know we were coming. Tommaseo took me aside and wanted me to tell him everything. He didn't start the interrogation until after the lawyer arrived, about half an hour later. All by the book."

"What did Arturo say in his own defense?"

"He kept insisting that he got to his father's house a little before eight, but Tommaseo summoned the bookseller and Modica, the neighbor, for this afternoon. He'll definitely crack with them there."

"Did he say anything that might be of interest to us?"

"He laid into his sister Giovanna," said Fazio.

"Called her a slut and a whore," said Mimì.

"And said she was her father's daughter," Fazio continued.

"What kind of accusation is that?"

"Meaning that as for taking lovers, she herself was no slouch," Mimì explained.

"Did he name any names?"

"Absolutely!" said Fazio, "The notary Piscopo himself, Lamantia the engineer, a lawyer named Di Stefano, Santo Fallace, who is a businessman dealing in pharmaceuticals—"

"What's that got to do with anything?" Montalbano interrupted him. "The fact that his sister had a lot of lovers doesn't mean he's not a murderer."

"That's true," said Mimì. "But he pointed out that they were all people whom his father knew and whom Giovanna used to make him look bad. He said that his father, by leaving the greater part of his inheritance to Giovanna, didn't do it because she had two children, but because he'd been prevailed upon by Giovanna and the friends of his who'd been her lovers."

In short, in front of the prosecutor, Arturo, mincing no words, had his revenge on Giovanna for the accusations she had made against him.

Quite a family, you had to admit! A nest of vipers might be a better description.

"Okay," Montalbano concluded. "Fazio, you can go and get started on your search."

Fazio said good-bye and went out.

"What search?" asked Augello.

"I'll tell you in a second. First you tell me what Barletta's letters to Alina were like."

"They're exactly like the girl said: awkward and ungrammatical. But they do show that he was genuinely in love with her. And he would definitely have made out the will in her favor. He'd lost his head over her. By that point the girl was the only thing in the world that mattered to him."

"So let's talk about some of the other love letters."

He took the packet of letters from the unknown girl and held it out to Augello.

"But I've already read them!"

"I want you to look at the passages I under-lined."

When Mimì had finished, the inspector said to him:

"Now, try and bear with me, Mimì. I'm going give a kind of summary. What emerges from these letters, first of all, is that Barletta knew this woman when she was a little girl; second, we learn that their relationship had its ups and downs; third, that their meetings were extremely risky; fourth, that in the meantime she's gone with another man; fifth, that they had a new opportunity to become lovers again; sixth, that she got pregnant from this and kept the child; seventh, that we're looking at an affair that lasted years and years; eighth, that the two shared another secret besides the fact of being lovers."

"That's a summary of past episodes. Now tell me what happens next."

"I've come to the conclusion that this woman must be the daughter of a very good friend of Barletta's, a friend who used to come to his house. And that's the research I want Fazio to do."

Mimì remained pensive.

"You don't agree?" the inspector asked.

"I completely agree. But I wonder why Barletta kept those letters."

"Aside from the fact that Barletta kept everything, those letters contain written, irrefutable proof that this woman had a child from him."

"Yeah, but what use to him was this proof?"

"How can anyone answer a question like that? You would have to go inside Barletta's soul to know. Which wouldn't be easy. Meanwhile it's clear that he was in love with this woman, but in his own way. It might have been his strategy for keeping her tied to him forever."

"How?"

"Mimì, say she threatened to leave him. He could blackmail her with this business of the child."

"But I got the impression that she was more in love with him than vice versa."

"That's quite right. So the question is this: How would a woman so in love react if she found out that the most important man in her life had gone head over heels over a twenty-year-old girl? That she'd been definitively replaced?"

"She might kill him."

"That's what I say too. And that's why I put Fazio to work."

"Wait a second. But if Barletta was so much in love with Alina, why did he spend his last night with another woman?"

"Well, the fact that he spent his last night with a woman is something we have inferred from the blond hair we found in the double bed, which had clearly been slept in by two people. But something Giovanna said makes me unsure."

"And what's that?"

"She said that her father didn't always make his bed. He would simply pull up the sheet or the blanket and then would leave it that way until the housekeeper came the next day. So it's not certain that the blond hair was from the night between Saturday and Sunday."

"That seems to make sense."

"Right. However, despite Giovanna's observation, one thing remains certain. That whoever killed him with poison at six in the morning is the same person who spent the night with him, I don't care if she's blonde or raven haired. They drank their morning coffee together, after they got up."

"But do you really believe that the person who poisoned him was the one who wrote the letters—who, don't forget, would be not only his longtime lover but also the mother of his child?"

"Yes. And I'll explain. You yourself were wondering why Barletta, though madly in love with Alina, would spend the night with another woman. There is only one possible answer to this question: It wasn't just any woman, but her, the one with whom he'd had a long, authentically passionate relationship until he met Alina."

"So what do you think happened?"

"Here's my theory. The old mistress discovers that Barletta has flipped irretrievably for Alina. This is tragic news to her, since up to then Barletta had only had brief affairs. But, mind you, she has always been jealous of these affairs, and she even repays him in kind, as she says in one letter. Are you with me so far?"

"I'm with you."

"This time, however, it's not some passing fancy we're talking about, but love, infatuation, senile dementia, call it what you will. The unknown woman's jealousy must have become unbearable, blinding. She says and does what she needs to do to get Barletta to allow her to come to his house on Saturday night. And she probably cries and despairs, but Barletta won't budge."

"There's an inconsistency here, Salvo. If Barletta didn't want to have anything more to do with her, how is it she ends up in bed with him?"

"Because it's inevitable. Don't forget what she wrote, though in different words. As soon as their bodies come into contact with each other, the passions are triggered. And they over-power everything else. That's what happened that night. But it's meaningless. The unknown woman knows that she'll have to leave the following morning, there are no two ways about it. She's brought her poison along with her, in case she should fail to change his mind. And she did fail, so she uses it. Make sense to you?"

"Makes sense to me," said Mimì Augello. "But what kind of poison was it?"

"Pasquano told me. It's a poison that paralyzes. Wait a second."

He dug around in all his pockets but didn't find the scrap of paper with the name the doctor had told him. The only hope was to ring Pasquano. He turned on the speakerphone.

"What's your latest excuse for busting my balls?" asked an angry Pasquano.

"I'm sorry, Doctor, but I lost the piece of paper I wrote the name of that poison on."

"Can't you see you're getting more senile with each day that goes by? Let's call it curanine. It's a by-product of curare. Haven't you ever read any adventure stories about the savages in the Amazon forest?"

"Yes, but why did you say 'let's call it'?"

"Because, though it is derived from curare—which, as I'm sure you don't know, paralyzes nerve endings—it's in very high concentration and can affect the respiratory system if ingested."

"Why? Does curare have no effect when ingested?"

"No. You can drink a whole glass of it. But if you're pricked with it—something I hope happens to you soon—you're a goner. And on that note, I wish you a pleasant evening," he concluded, and then hung up.

"You forgot to ask him something," said Mimì. "Whether it's easy to find."

"I'd already asked him. Pasquano said it's used in hospitals for treating things like rabies and epilepsy . . ."

All of a sudden he started laughing. Augello looked at him in perplexity.

"What's with you?"

"It's just that Arturo, by shooting his father, must have sent the real killer's plans up in smoke. She used a special poison that leaves no outward signs. It's quite possible she was counting on the fact that the doctor who eventually declared him dead would attribute it to natural causes. And so nobody would ever have known that Barletta was murdered. But then along comes Arturo and, not knowing he's already dead, he shoots him, thereby making an autopsy necessary. With the result that the coroner discovers cyanurine or whatever it's called in the body. And the killer, who was hoping to remain in the shadows, is screwed."

"She won't be screwed till we catch her," said Mimì. And he continued: "In conclusion, all we can do is hope Fazio comes through."

"There may be another way."

"How?"

"For me to talk to Giovanna. It's possible the unknown woman was a childhood friend of hers. It's possible they remained friends and still see each other."

"So why don't you talk to her?"

"Mimì, does this seem like the right moment to you? The very day we've arrested her brother? It's true she herself didn't refrain from casting suspicion on Arturo, but, come on . . ."

"I'd do it anyway . . . ," said Augello, going out.

The inspector sat there for a few minutes, thinking, weighing the pros and cons, then decided to take Mimì's advice. It was half past four. He dialed the number. She answered.

"Montalbano here. How are you?"

"How do you expect? How would you be if this . . . this terrible thing happened to you? My father murdered by my brother, his son! No . . . I really didn't think Arturo could ever do such a thing!"

"Listen, Giovanna, I realize it's not the best time to call, but—"

"Why? Do you mean because Arturo was arrested?"

"Well, yes."

"You were only doing your job. Why did you call?"

"Are you busy at the moment?"

"Not at all. I sent the children to their grand-parents' house for lunch, and my husband is out. I just wanted to be alone. Tell me."

"I need to talk to you."

She seemed to hesitate ever so slightly.

"Then come."

"Thank you. Please give me the address."

He'd just hung up when the phone rang.

"Ahh, Chief! 'Ere'd be yer ladygoilfrenn' onna line 'oo wants a talk t'yiz poissonally in poisson!"

Livia was calling him at the office at this hour?

"Did you go and see Mario? I called because, in case you haven't gone yet . . ."

Damn! He'd forgotten yet again! And he didn't know if he would find the time to go. The only way out was to lie.

"Come on, I promised you I'd go! Is that how you think of me? As someone who doesn't keep his word?"

"All right then, I'm sorry. How was he?"

"Just fine. He's completely recovered. And he sends you his warmest regards."

Some ten minutes later he was able to leave for Giovanna's.

When he saw her he felt uneasy. She wasn't the same Giovanna as last time. She was disheveled and hadn't made herself up, and she had dark circles under her eyes and lines on both sides of her unsmiling lips. It was clear that the sort of Greek tragedy that had occurred in her family had left its mark on her.

"It's been a terrible day," she said as she was showing the inspector into the living room. "These journalists are a plague! They're vultures, hyenas! They won't stop calling! They won't even let me catch my breath! They're running me into the ground!"

"And now it's my turn," said Montalbano.

"No, you're different," said Giovanna, with no hint of a smile.

She sat down in an armchair opposite him.

"I'll try my best to bother you as little as possible," the inspector began.

He took the unknown woman's letters out of his jacket pocket.

"These letters were found in a secret drawer of your father's desk. I want you to look at them."

"I've already seen them," she said.

Montalbano was astonished.

"When?"

"That evening I came to the police station, remember? You had them on your desk. Actually, one of them fell to the floor and—"

"But did you have a chance to read them?"

"No."

"Can I ask you to do so now?"

"All right. Would you like some whisky?"

"Yes, thanks."

She read as he drank. At a certain point large tears started rolling down her face. She wept in silence.

"If it's too painful for you . . ."

She shook her head no. When she'd finished, she set the letters down on the coffee table and stood up.

"Excuse me just a minute."

She returned several minutes later, having washed her face and combed her hair.

"Do you feel up to talking?"

"Yes."

"What do you think?"

"That that was the only woman who truly loved Papa."

"Any ideas?"

"Who she might be? No, none whatsoever. Anyway, how could I?"

"Well, that's just it, you see. Since the woman, in one letter, remembers your father taking her to the circus when she was still a little girl, I thought maybe you might have known her when you were a child."

"Wait . . . I do remember a time . . . when Papa took me to the circus too. I was . . . yes, I was four years old. Now that you've got me thinking about it . . ."

She trailed off, and a line appeared in the middle of her brow.

"Yes, there was another girl, the same age as me, but I can't seem to . . ."

"Please try and remember. We really need to know."

"Why?"

"Because I'm convinced that this little girl, after she grew up and became your father's mistress, is the one who poisoned him."

"Why would she have done that if she loved him so much?"

"You just said it yourself: *because* she loved him, and she couldn't stand the idea that your father—"

"—fell head over heels for a twenty-year-old. I get it."

Something didn't quite add up for Montalbano.

"Who told you your father fell head over heels for a young girl?"

She answered without hesitation.

"My father's lawyer told me when I talked to him over the phone. Listen, I'm sorry I can't help you with this, but—"

"Wait, just a minute more. I've ordered Fazio, whom you've met, to draw up a list of your father's friends, the ones who used to come to see him at home. If you could give me a few names, that would save us some time."

"I'd be glad to. The first names that come to mind are Piscopo the notary, Di Stefano the lawyer, and Lamantia the engineer. But . . ."

"But?"

"Piscopo never got married, Di Stefano has two sons, and only Lamantia has a daughter my age. Her name is Anna. Listen . . ."

"Yes?"

"Can I keep these letters? I would like to look at them more closely. They might help jog my memory . . ."

"All right, but . . ."

"Don't worry, I'll give them back."

As he was leaving Giovanna's apartment, he sensed that the investigation had finally arrived at something concrete. And he also felt, for no apparent reason, that he had no time to waste. He had his cell phone in his pocket and used it to call Fazio.

"See you in twenty minutes, at the office."

"What is it, Chief?"

"Did you find out who Barletta's close friends—"

"Chief, there was nothing to find out. Arturo

had already listed them for Tommaseo. Piscopo, Di Stefano, Fallace, Lamantia—who he said was his sister Giovanna's lover."

"Right, Lamantia. He has a daughter named Anna who—"

"Lamantia is the very person I started with."

"Were you able to find out anything about this Anna?"

"Yeah, Chief. She's gravely ill and has been in a Palermo clinic for almost a month."

Montalbano was crestfallen. Yet another lead gone to the dogs.

Then why had Giovanna mentioned her name to him?

On his way home, he stopped the car at the start of the path that led up to the hobo's cave, got out, and began climbing. But the man wasn't there; apparently he wasn't back yet. So if he'd gone out, it meant he felt all right. The lie Montalbano had told Livia tallied with the truth. With his heart at peace, he went back to the car, turned it around, and went home. Naturally, as he was unlocking the door, he heard the phone ringing.

"Hi, Salvo, it's Mimì."

"What is it?"

"We just got a call from Tommaseo's office. Arturo has confessed. It all happened the way you thought it did. He knew that the notary was coming to the house that morning to change the will, because Barletta—who was also a sadist on top of everything else—had told him. Or, actually, it wasn't to change the will, but to make a final version of the draft that Barletta had already prepared."

"He'd prepared a draft?"

"That's what he said. And so he wanted to prevent him. He got there at a quarter to seven, unlocked the door with his own key, saw his father sitting in the kitchen taking his morning coffee, and shot him. Then he started looking for the draft of the new will. But he couldn't find it. We couldn't find it either, for that matter. And that's the story. Ah, I almost forgot: Arturo had buried the gun, and so a team went to dig it up."

He hardly touched the food Adelina had cooked for him. He sat out on the veranda, smoking and thinking, feeling quite uneasy. Deep inside he felt he'd missed something in the overall picture, some detail that merited greater attention. But what? And at what moment of the investigation?

He felt like drinking a little whisky, but wouldn't allow himself. His head had to remain clear.

All at once, and without knowing why, something Augello had said to him over the phone came back to him—namely, that Arturo had known about the change in the will because his father himself had told him, out of sheer sadism. And he must have also told him the reason for the change: that he'd fallen in love with a twenty-year-old girl. His sister Giovanna, on the other hand, based on what she'd told him, only knew about her father's affair with the girl because the lawyer, Alfano, had just told her that same day. And in so saying she implied that she'd been in the dark about both the change in the will and the reason for the change.

But this was the very thing that didn't make sense!

Even assuming that Giovanna hadn't known the reason, she couldn't not have known about the change. How could her father have communicated it to Arturo without also telling his daughter, with whom he was on closer terms? And even if Barletta didn't tell her, how was it possible Arturo wouldn't have told her of their father's intentions? And it was Giovanna herself, the first time the inspector had seen her, who told him that Arturo feared this exact scenario! Therefore her brother would have immediately called her up and said something to the effect of "You see? I was right!"

No, he was absolutely certain that Giovanna, too, was aware of the situation. And therefore, if she knew, how was it possible she hadn't talked about it with her father, in hopes of making him change his mind?

Okay, but so what? So she talked to him about it and he remained firm in his intentions.

He was going round in circles. It was best to banish Giovanna from his thoughts and go back to thinking about the unknown woman's letters.

18

But at that moment the telephone rang. It was Livia, calling to say good night. She asked him how the investigation was going, and he told her that Arturo had confessed.

"What a relief!"

"Why?"

"Because now you'll have no more reason to meet with that woman, who's in the habit of saying good-bye a little too affectionately."

He didn't tell her he'd actually gone out to dinner with her and was still meeting with her, though she was no longer in the habit of kissing him. After a brief chat they said good night, miraculously without having quarreled.

When he sat back down on the veranda, he remembered the scene when Livia slapped him. He started laughing, but suddenly stopped.

Just one second, Montalbà! Hold it right there!

You can't just shut Giovanna out of your thoughts! In fact, let's backtrack a little.

Why had Giovanna so insistently wanted to go back to her father's house?

She'd pulled out that story of wanting to recover the diamond ring before the house was reopened . . .

266

Maybe the best thing was to try to remember everything they did during the time they were at the house. So, he removed the seals, she unlocked the door, they went inside, the light switch didn't work, she opened the shutters to one window, they went upstairs, she went into the bathroom and opened the shutter, and she realized the ring wasn't on the sink as Mimì had said. And so he rang Mimì, who explained that he'd been mistaken; he'd actually put the ring under some shirts in the top drawer of the armoire. Giovanna, who'd overheard the exchange, quickly ran out of the room while he stayed behind to wipe his brow and shut the shutter. Then he went into the guest room, but Giovanna wasn't there, because Mimì had meant the armoire in Barletta's bedroom. When he went in, he saw the armoire open, the drawer with the shirts half pulled out, and Giovanna holding the little box with the ring. And what, by the way, was the jeweler's name? Ah, yes: Marco Falzone. From Montelusa.

At this point he could venture a hypothesis. Giovanna learns from her brother that there's a draft of a new will. A highly dangerous document, which must be gotten rid of. She also knows that neither Arturo nor the police have been able to find it. She thinks about this and has an idea where her father may have hidden it in the house. But she can't get inside. So, using the ring as an excuse, she has him take down the seals, goes inside, and taking advantage of the moment she's left alone, she grabs not only the ring, but also the old will, if it's still there, and the draft of the new one. And sayonara to one and all.

Thus, with Arturo in jail (with she herself having helped to send him there with her insinuations against him, even in their second meeting) and with no form of will any longer in existence, Signora Giovanna becomes the sole heir to the estate. Not a bad plan. Congratulations. And he, Inspector Montalbano, noted for his acumen and lightning intuitions, had actually lent her a hand! Heartfelt compliments to him as well. He deserved not just one slap in the face, but a hundred thousand!

He felt so enraged that he went and got a bottle of whisky and a glass, brought them out to the veranda, and started drinking. He would go back to Giovanna's in the morning and scare the living daylights out of her.

Despite having knocked back half the bottle, he couldn't fall asleep. The hours passed without his even noticing. He tormented himself, stewed in his juices, cursed himself, thought Pasquano was right to repeat the constant refrain that he was getting too old for his job. The image of the puppet he'd become in Giovanna's hands burned in his mind like live fire. At the same time, he realized that she could quite easily defend herself

268

from the accusation. It was simply a hypothesis with no evidence to support it. He had no proof of anything. How was he ever going to catch her?

As for having no proof of anything, he also had nothing that might help to identify the real killer, the woman who poisoned Barletta. Maybe he should start all over again and look at everything from another perspective. *Never mind who the killer is; let's ask ourselves how she was able to get her hands on a poison found only in hospitals . . .*

Among all of Barletta's many girlfriends, was there one who was the daughter of a doctor, pharmacist, or nurse?

Wait, Montalbà, wait! Wasn't there some moment in which someone had said something about a pharmacy or something similar?

Yes, he was sure of it. But when? And who'd said it?

Without realizing what he was doing, he got up, went into the other room, grabbed the phone, and called Fazio. He had to wait a long time before somebody picked up.

"Chief, what is it?"

"Were you asleep?"

"Chief, it's five o'clock in the morning!"

He looked at his watch. It was true! But since he'd already woken him up, might as well not make him lose sleep for no reason.

"I apologize, but . . . listen, in connection

269

with the Barletta case, do you remember anyone saying something about a pharmacist or
pharmacy?"

"No, I really don't."

Was it possible he'd dreamt it?

"Anything about doctors, hospitals, emergency
rooms . . . ?"

"No, Chief. The only person having anything to
do with medicine is Santo Fallace, who owns a
small pharmaceutical company in Montelusa . . ."

The flash that went off in Montalbano's head
seemed to light up the whole room. Well, what
a coincidence! The very name Giovanna didn't
mention when listing her father's friends! She'd
left it out on purpose! Because he was also one of
her lovers!

Montalbano's legs started to give out. He
grabbed a chair and sat down.

"You still there, Chief?"

He had trouble opening his mouth.

"Yeah, I'm still here. Listen, in three hours, at
eight o'clock, I want Fallace in my office."

*No, Montalbà, fight it with all your might, close
off every passage in your mind to the horrific
thought trying to force its way past every barrier
you put up. Don't leave open the slightest nook,
crack, or fissure, or you'll plunge into a hellish
abyss.*

Numb yourself, finish the whisky left in the

bottle, get drunk, or else go down to the beach and bury your head in the sand so as not to see or hear anything, the way ostriches do . . .

But he was unable to keep from falling into the abyss.

As hc was dashing to the shower, having suddenly felt as greasy as if a jerrican's worth of machine oil had spilled all over him, he heard, very close by, a bird singing. A bird singing fanciful variations on the theme of "Il cielo in una stanza." He stopped short. What was this nonsense? He'd heard that melody before. Was it in the dream about Yadwigha's forest? But he was awake now! No, that couldn't be it. Then he suddenly realized it was Mario, the vagabond, who was whistling. He ran out to the veranda.

"Good morning. I saw you were awake, and so . . . I came to say hello. And to tell you something. I'm leaving."

"Why?"

"You'll understand after I tell you what I came here to tell you . . ."

"Listen, come with me into the kitchen. I'll make some coffee."

The vagabond followed him. Montalbano sat him down and went and bustled about with the Neapolitan coffeepot.

"So, tell me."

"Years ago, I used to sleep in a hayloft from

which you could see Barletta's house below. It was on a hilltop, behind the road . . . and only about a hundred yards from the house."

"Go on."

"One morning, the sixth of July, to be precise—another date of my life I'll never forget—at around ten o'clock or so, I was heading down towards the road when I heard a terrible, heartrending, desperate scream. A moment later Signora Barletta—whom I knew well—came running out of the house, towards the sea, screaming as she ran, and as she screamed she took off her dressing gown and nightshirt and threw them down on the sand . . . And she ran into the sea, still screaming. I stood there, not moving, not knowing what to do, not understanding what was happening . . . And then I saw Giovanna come out of the house, half-naked, and then, a moment later, her father appeared in a bathing suit . . . They stood there for a few seconds, frozen like statues, and then Barletta grabbed his daughter by the arm and pulled her back into the house. By this point the woman's screams had become almost inaudible, and she was little more than a faraway dot in the water . . . Only then was I able to race down the hillside, cross the road, run onto the beach, dive into the water . . . I'm . . . I used to be a good swimmer. But when I got there . . . I couldn't see her anymore. And so I went down, underwater, and looked around, and at last I spotted her . . . I realized at once that I'd got there too late. I am, or I used to be, a surgeon. At any rate I managed to drag her to the shore and try mouth-to-mouth resuscitation on her, but it was all for naught. I left her there and ran quickly away. That same day I went to live somewhere else."

"Why?"

"I didn't want anyone to . . . be able to identify me. The paper said it was a terrible accident. That's not true, Inspector. It was a suicide. Which those two could have prevented, but didn't."

We made a lightning decision that terrible day. Do you remember?

Without saying a word, without exchanging a glance, we acted in unison and let things take their course . . .

To climb out of the abyss, where he couldn't breathe . . . To rise up wildly, desperately, pretending not to have heard what Mario had told him, and then to pour the coffee and ask:

"How much sugar?"

"One, please," said Mario, looking at him with incomprehension, since there seemed to be no reason for the inspector's lack of reaction.

While he, politely, as though sitting at a café table:

"Forgive me for asking," he said, "but why did you decide . . . if you were a . . ."

Mario understood at once.

"I made a tragic mistake. I killed a small child in the operating room. I was acquitted by the courts, but I knew I was guilty. Because I was distracted. I'd been thinking about my wife, who was cheating on me . . . I was no longer able to . . . I let myself go. You see?"

He smiled wanly.

"You're already starting."

"Starting what?"

"To ask questions. That's why I'm leaving."

He stood up and held out his hand to the inspector.

"Anyway, as you'll understand, given my personal situation, I'm in no position to testify. Please give my fond regards to Signora Livia. Take good care of her."

He gave a sort of half bow, turned his back, and went out.

And now that you're alone, Montalbà, you have no choice but to descend once again into the abyss. You cannot refuse. It's your job as a cop. Your curse.

Try, however, to do it without experiencing the vertigo one feels when peering all the way to the bottom. Make your way down there carefully, with eyes closed, one step at a time . . .

274

"I am carrying your baby inside me."

So how would one call this baby that was both the child and grandchild of the same man? Child and sibling of the same woman? Even Barletta had sensed the horror of it, but not her. Not her.

"I have decided to pay you back in kind. Your affairs are driving me insane with jealousy . . ."

And she'd kept her promise, taking on all her father's friends as lovers! One after another, with cold calculation. And maybe she'd even told him, to make him jealous in turn . . .

"We made a lightning decision . . ."

To let their respective wife and mother commit suicide, probably after she'd caught them together . . . It was bound to happen sooner or later. Giovanna herself had said that their meetings were extremely risky . . .

"I remember when I was a little girl and you took me to the circus . . ."

But when did the two of them become lovers? Three years later? When the girl was seven? Or eight? Or ten?

He must have made a false step, because Montalbano's fall into an endless void of darkness and terror was sudden and precipitous.

Trembling, he laid his forehead down on the wooden desktop and stayed that way for a long time, still falling.

"Bring him in," he said to Fazio.

Also present was Augello, who, upon seeing him walk into headquarters, asked him:

"What's wrong, have you got a fever?"

"No."

Santo Fallace was a man of about sixty who was keen to stay in shape and dress well. He looked worried.

"Signor Fallace, do you own a pharmaceutical firm?"

"Yes. In Montelusa."

"Did you know that your friend Cosimo Barletta was killed with a paralyzing poison that is used only in hospitals?"

"Yes."

"Does your firm produce this substance?"

"Yes. In small quantities."

"Do you know Giovanna Barletta?"

Fallace showed his first signs of uneasiness.

"I was a friend of her father's."

"My question was of a different nature. Have you had intimate relations with the woman?"

"Well . . . yes."

"When?"

"Well, they've been . . . sporadic."

"When was the last time?"

"A little over a month ago."

"Did she ever happen to visit your establishment?"

"Yes, she's been there at least three times."

"When was the last time?"

"Exactly a month ago."

"And did she make any particular requests on that occasion?"

"I don't . . . I don't understand."

"Did the woman ask you for any medicine without a normal prescription?"

Fallace's unease and concern condensed into a few drops of sweat on his brow.

"Yes. Since her son Cosimo . . ."

She'd given him the same name!

". . . suffers from epilepsy . . . she asked me to give her . . ."

". . . a phial of the same poison that . . ."

". . . but I told her that if used incorrectly it was a deadly poison!" Fallace burst out. "That you had to dilute it with . . . and she assured me that . . ."

"All right, you can go."

More surprised than Fallace himself at Montalbano's words were Augello and Fazio.

"Thank you. Have a good day," said Fallace, standing up and running away.

"So you let him go, just like that?" asked a puzzled Augello.

"So it was Giovanna!" an astonished Fazio said instead.

"Yes, Giovanna did it," Montalbano confirmed.

"So we can go immediately and—" Fazio began.

"No, not yet," the inspector said firmly.

"But don't you know what Fallace is doing at this very moment?" Augello protested. "He's calling Giovanna to warn her! We have no time to lose!"

"Calm down, Mimì, she won't run away. She has nowhere to go. I have to make a phone call first."

Fazio started glaring at him, while Mimì stormed out of the room, upset. Montalbano picked up the receiver.

"Cat, get me Marco Falzone Jewelers on the line and put the call through to me, would you?"

"Falzone Jewelers. How may I help you?"

He turned on the speakerphone.

"This is Inspector Montalbano, police. I want to know who it was that bought a woman's ring from you with a circle of diamonds in the middle."

"When?"

"I really don't know."

"Inspector, you must realize that with so little information . . ."

"I understand. I could give you the name of a possible buyer."

"That would already be something."

"Cosimo Barletta."

"Please wait while I search the computer . . . Yes, here he is. He's the very man who bought it. Eight months ago. I'm sorry, but isn't Barletta the man who was . . . ?"

"Thank you," said Montalbano, hanging up.

"And now that you've stalled for as long as it was possible to stall," said Fazio, "can we go?"

"Let's go."

"Shall I inform Inspector Augello?"

"Never mind."

"Is Signora Giovanna Barletta at home?" Montalbano asked the concierge.

"She hasn't gone out yet this morning."

They knocked and knocked at the door, but nobody came.

"Go downstairs and see if the concierge has an extra key."

While waiting, he fired up a cigarette. Now he was certain that Giovanna had made good use of the time he'd granted her. Fazio returned with the key. They unlocked the door and went in.

Giovanna was lying on the bed, lifeless.

In her hand was a small, empty phial.

She'd killed herself with the same poison.

On her bedside table was a note written in a steady hand.

Inspector Montalbano, after getting a call from Santo Fallace, I had no other choice. You figured it all out. I'm sorry, but I had to destroy the letters. I ask you please to do what's best. I did what I did, it should be clear, to have the whole inheritance to myself. Thank you.

He now realized that the whole affair had to be seen in a different light. Except that the word that defined it was very hard to pronounce.

"You never saw this note," he said to Fazio as he put it in his pocket.

". . . maybe she spends the night trying to persuade her father, but doesn't succeed. So they go to bed, each in his or her own room. Giovanna gets up early. She has to head back to Montelusa by six at the latest. She takes a shower, goes down into the kitchen to make coffee. Then Barletta, after splashing a little water on himself, also goes downstairs and sits down at the table. Giovanna pours him the poison coffee, then drinks her own and washes her cup. She leaves, locking the door behind her. She has achieved her goal. She has prevented her father from changing the will. Maybe she takes a different road home, so as not to cross paths with her brother's car. By six-thirty she's in Montelusa. She carefully opens her front door, gets undressed, and goes and wakes up the nanny. A little later she goes and wakes up the children as well. Arturo's call telling her that their father's been shot must have upset her, since it makes her plan to have the death appear to have been a natural one go up in smoke. And that's the story."

"Good God, what a family!" exclaimed

Tommaseo. "A brother and sister who kill their parent over a sordid question of self-interest!"

"Yeah," said Montalbano.

As Giovanna had indirectly implored him in her note, he would never tell the prosecutor the truth.

"I ask you please to do what's best."

Because, for her, at least, there was no question of self-interest. She didn't give a damn about wills and testaments.

And she had, in fact, gone back to the house to recover the ring, the last present given her by the man she loved.

It was love.

Could one really use the word? If you could overcome the disgust, the nausea, the horror, and get at the substance, then, maybe, yes. You could use the word, but only deep inside your own heart. Not with others.

Desperate, unnatural, incestuous, horrific, inconceivable, repulsive, scandalous, degenerate . . . All the adjectives you want.

But still a kind of love.

No, it was pointless to tell Tommaseo what had really happened.

"Love!" the prosecutor would have fired back. "You call this . . . ignoble animality, you call that love?"

But what else could you call it?

281

Author's Note

The novel you have in your hands was written in 2008.

At the time, its publication was postponed because the story was too similar to that of *The Paper Moon*, published in 2004, in which I didn't have the courage to fully develop the theme of incest, always a difficult subject to treat.

I do hope that nobody will claim to recognize him- or herself in this story, which is entirely the fruit of my imagination.

Notes

5–6 ***The Dream*** **. . . Yadwigha:** Henri Rousseau's *The Dream* is also known sometimes as *Yadwigha's Dream,* as the woman represented in it is supposed to be Yadwigha, Rousseau's first mistress.

6 **Mina:** Mina (born Anna Maria Mazzini in 1940) is a major Italian pop music diva who has worked in many genres. "Il cielo in una stanza" was one of her many hit songs; the title means "The Sky in a Room."

29 **Did he have a notary:** In Italy, as in many other European countries, notaries are lawyers employed by the state and are in charge of many of the legal procedures concerning civil status, including last will and testament.

40 **Stella Lasorella:** *La sorella,* in Italian, means "the sister."

104 **"But there aren't any more insane asylums!":** In 1978, the passage of Law 180 (also known as the Franco Basaglia Law, after the famous psychiatrist-neurologist who inspired it) technically abolished insane asylums in Italy. Among other things, it eliminated "dangerousness" as an acceptable reason for treatment. It

283

did stipulate, however, that "obligatory mental health treatment" (*Trattamento Sanitario Obligatorio*, or TSO) must be applied to individuals whose "psychological disturbances are such as to require urgent therapy," if such therapy is not voluntarily accepted by the persons in question. Care to the mentally ill would be provided by a variety of institutions, including outpatient clinics, community centers, and "residential" and "semiresidential" centers. Law 180 was slow in being applied. The first Berlusconi government moved in 1994 to close the remaining sanatoriums still open. But, as it turns out, the current system makes available to patients far more psychiatric services than before; the "residential centers" are, in effect, psychiatric hospitals. The inflexibly coercive nature of the pre-1978 asylums has, however, been considerably diminished.

130 **If the carabinieri intervened, the whole thing was sure to end in farce:** In Italy the carabinieri, a national police force under the jurisdiction of the military, are commonly viewed as short on intelligence and are therefore often the butt of jokes. They are also often in competition with the regular local police forces, and Montalbano in particular usually prefers to steer clear of them.

147 **They say that D'Annunzio used to keep specimens of pubic hair . . . :** Gabriele D'Annunzio (1863–1938), a celebrated poet of diminutive stature and great bluster, was reputed to be sexually insatiable and given to strange erotic practices.

165 ***Sing, goddess, the anger of Peleus' son Achilleus . . . :*** This, and the quoted passage that follows, are from the Richmond Lattimore translation, University of Chicago Press, 1951.

170 **Inspector Mazzancolla:** *Mazzancolla* is a kind of Mediterranean prawn. Catarella later makes the same mistake as Montalbano, calling Mazzacolla Mazzancolla.

174 **". . . also a middical dacter?":** In Italy, Montalbano's title of *commissario di pubblica sicurezza* ("Commissar of Public Safety") requires a university degree, and any full university degree confers on its recipient the title of *dottore*, or "doctor." Indeed, in the original versions of these stories, Montalbano's colleagues often call him *"dottore."*

178 **". . . and without suspicion," . . . Dante:** Montalbano is quoting from Dante's *Inferno* (canto 5, 1.129), *"senza alcun sospetto,"* in reference to the story of illicit love between

Paolo Malatesta and Francesca da Rimini, which earned the famous couple a place in the second circle of hell among the lustful.

196 **. . . as fake as the Modigliani heads that were found in Livorno.** In 1984, on the occasion of the one hundredth anniversary of the birth of Italian modernist painter Amedeo Modigliani (1884–1920), some local artists got the idea to drum up a little excitement. As described in the May 20, 2014, issue of thelocal.it (http://www .thelocal.it/20140520/livorno-plans-to -show-fake-modigliani-heads), an English-language news webzine for Italy:

It was the summer of 1984, and an exhibition to commemorate the 100th anniversary of Modigliani's birth in his hometown had begun on a lacklustre note.

So in an effort to drum up more enthusiasm, the organizer, Vera Durbé, decided to fund a search for the carved heads that Modigliani is said to have hurled into the Fosse Reale canal after receiving negative reviews.

A week into the search, three sculptures were found at the bottom of the canal, prompting Durbé to announce they were Modigliani originals, a declaration that attracted hundreds of visitors to the city.

But art historian Federico Zeri cast doubt on their authenticity, saying they were so "immature" that Modigliani had been right to cast them aside.

The three students later confessed to producing one of them with a Black & Decker drill, while the other two were made by a local artist.

Notes by Stephen Sartarelli

Andrea Camilleri, a bestseller in Italy and Germany, is the author of the popular Inspector Montalbano mystery series as well as historical novels that take place in nineteenth-century Sicily. His books have been made into Italian TV shows and translated into thirty-two languages. His thirteenth Montalbano novel, *The Potter's Field*, won the Crime Writers' Association International Dagger Award and was longlisted for the IMPAC Dublin Literary Award.

Stephen Sartarelli is an award-winning translator and the author of three books of poetry.

Center Point Large Print
600 Brooks Road / PO Box 1
Thorndike, ME 04986-0001 USA

(207) 568-3717

US & Canada:
1 800 929-9108
www.centerpointlargeprint.com